Chinese Nights Entertainments

Also from Westphalia Press
westphaliapress.org

Chinese Nights Entertainments

Stories of Old China

Selected and edited by
Brian Brown

Foward by
Sao-ke Alfred Sze

WESTPHALIA PRESS
An imprint of Policy Studies Organization

Westphalia Press
An imprint of Policy Studies Organization
1527 New Hampshire Ave., NW
Washington, D.C. 20036
info@ipsonet.org

ISBN-13: 978-1-63391-240-3
ISBN-10: 163391240X

Cover design by Jeffrey Barnes:
www.jbarnesdesign.com

Daniel Gutierrez-Sandoval, Executive Director
PSO and Westphalia Press

Updated material and comments on this edition
can be found at the Westphalia Press website:
www.westphaliapress.org

CHINESE NIGHTS ENTERTAINMENTS

Stories of Old China

SELECTED AND EDITED BY
BRIAN BROWN

FOREWORD BY
SAO-KE ALFRED SZE
Chinese Minister to the United States

ILLUSTRATED

NEW YORK
BRENTANO'S
Publishers

THE HOME OF KNO TZU CHIEN, CHINESE SAGE
AT THE STORY TELLING HOUR.

Chinese Nights Entertainments

Stories of Old China

FOREWORD

In the old quaint tea houses by the roadside or the crowded houseboats on their way to the temple, the Chinese, since time immemorial, had the habit, like the people in the time of Chaucer, of telling stories. Some would narrate their own experiences, while others would simply repeat what they had committed to memory since their childhood. These tales were handed down from one generation to another until they became a part and parcel of the nation's culture and life.

Fantastic and mysterious, these fables were originally intended for entertainment. As time went on, however, greater significance was attached to them. Leslie Stephen spoke of Horace Walpole's *"Castle of Otranto"*: "Absurd as the burlesque seems, our ancestors found it amusing, and, what is stranger, awe-inspiring." The same might be said of the stories collected in this volume.

Fiction is not necessarily entirely devoid of truth. Practically in every one of these stories, one will find bits of information about China's custom, manners, history, and even philosophy. Their grotesqueness never mars their theme; and, like the Fables of Æsop or Le Fontaine, each of them imparts a moral. Chinese hedonism is never perfect without a lesson.

In the days of old, novels and short stories had no recognized place in Chinese literature. The old literati never aspired to be a story teller. Time has changed and now the bookstores in China are literally flooded with stories. A fairly educated man is supposed to be familiar with the works of Chehkov, Maupassant, and Kipling.

It is quite noticeable that the American public is taking a deeper interest in Chinese literature now than they ever did before. The mysterious East is gradually revealing itself to the Occident. Miss Amy Lowell's recent translations of Chinese poems have been very favorably received by the reading public in this country, and I am quite certain that Mr. Brown's present collection will be accorded an equally warm reception.

SAO-KE ALFRED SZE

June 8, 1922
Washington, D. C.

ACKNOWLEDGMENTS AND SOURCES

I wish to acknowledge my indebtedness to the following publishers and authors, for their kind permission to print in this volume, copyright material from their publications.

The Fleming H. Revell Co., 158 Fifth Avenue, New York City, for the privilege of including the story "The Chinese Hero" from their publication called "Gleaning from Chinese Folk Lore" by N. R. Russell.

Brentano's, 225 Fifth Avenue, New York City, for the privilege to include the "Taoist Explanation of Love" taken from their publication "Laotzu's Tao and Wu Wei."

John Murray of London, and E. P. Dutton of New York for the use of four tales from "The Taoist Teaching" in the Wisdom of the East Series. "The Woodgather" and the other tales in the "Chinese Nights Entertainers" are from "A String of Chinese Peach-Stones" by W. Arthur Cornaby and published by Charles H. Kelly, London. "The Daughter of Sun Hou" is taken from an old volume called "The Porcelain Tower" translated from original sources and published in London in 1840,—this work is long out of print.

T. Werner Laurie, Ltd., London, for the use of some stories from Herbert A. Giles, "Strange Stories from A Chinese Studio." While the arrangement of the tales in this volume is my own, and though I have changed the structure of many of them materially, the rewriting was always done with the assistance of some Chinese friends and the original sense of the tales preserved in every case.

ACKNOWLEDGMENTS AND SOURCES

I wish to express my thanks to these, my Chinese friends, who are so modest that they do not wish their names mentioned. I also wish to thank Sao-Ke Alfred Sze, Minister from China to United States, for his kindness in writing a foreword for these tales, and for giving suggestions that helped the effort greatly.

BRIAN BROWN

CONTENTS

PART I

CHINESE NIGHTS ENTERTAINMENTS

PART II

TAOIST TALES

CONTENTS

PART III

THE FEAST OF LANTERNS

ILLUSTRATIONS

PART I

Chinese Nights Entertainments

Chinese Nights Entertainment

IN a small country town in China there lived
a great scholar named Kno Tzu Chien. This
sage was an authority upon the old classics, and
he also loved the folklore and fairy tales of
ancient China. On winter evenings the home
of this greatly loved scholar was a popular
gathering place, and many of the old folks,
from near and far, came and told folk tales
that had been told to them in their youth—
tales of old China that had been handed down
from generation to generation in the same way
—told at the firesides. Kno Tzu Chien presided
over all these gatherings, (which might be called
"Chinese Nights Entertainments"), and during
the evenings would consult several old books,
so as to give an accurate and detailed account
of the interesting history and legendary lore
which belongs to old China.

The evening's entertainment usually begins by
each guest receiving a cup of scented tea. A red
unglazed earthen kettle is heard singing on the

fire in the adjoining kitchen—so the company can be assured of plenty more before the night's batch of tales are told. On the cook fire are pans full of home-made cakes, slightly salted; these are to be eaten warm. They will give joy to the young folks—when the night's stories are half told. With tea cups at hand, more tea in prospect, and the savoury prophecy exhaled from such cakes, there is complete satisfaction among the company gathered, to partake of the evening's intellectual feast. Kno Tzu Chien is seated upon a high chair, with his right hand towards the door, so that all who enter may be given the customary salutation befitting their station.

Before the story telling begins Kno Tzu Chien orders three sticks of incense lighted and the foxes of the place worshipped—for the fox occupies a very high place in Chinese folklore—then he calls upon some one to tell a tale of the fox in Chinese lore.

THE WICKED EMPRESS

Told By

MO TI FAH

All here know that the fox is regarded as far more than a mere beast. It has wondrous powers of transformation. While, according to Ancient lore, you can never be quite sure that your pet fox is not after all your grandfather, or some one else's, according to the popular notions. You cannot tell whether your visitor from a distance, or even the wife of your bosom, is not a transmogrified fox. The fox, or is it the foxen (the old non-technical form of the word vixen?) is specially addicted to taking the form of beautiful women, often to prove very "vixen" after all. The last monarch of the Yin (or Sha) dynasty (R. 1154–1122 B. C.), who, "Having lost the hearts of the people, could not appear before God, "had a wife yet more infamous than himself. This woman united to peerless beauty and consummate witchery the most inhuman passion for deeds of cruelty. A noble statesman's heart was cut out to see the colour thereof; folks' legs were amputated to see what it was that made some endure the cold so well. In short, the Emperor, at her instigation, undertook a series of vivisection experiments, in which the victims operated upon were human beings. This Ta Ki, as her name was, also invented copper cylinders, round which the victim was secured, fire being applied to make the tube red-hot. All of which is now explained on the theory that as the beautiful and innocent girl was on the way to the Capital, a specially malicious old fox killed her, assumed her form, and impersonated her ever afterwards. There, Mo Ti Fah added, that, if the story be true, that old fox is responsible for some of the finest poems in the Book of Odes, which were written to express the admiring gratitude of a people rescued from such enormities by the half-deified Literary King and his son the Military Monarch. "But among those old poems," he said, "foxes are only mentioned as 'solitary and suspicious'; their fur, together with lamb's skin, being made into winter robes for the courtiers." One poem speaks of "fox furs so yellow," another says, "Our fox furs are frayed and worn." The down on the fox's ribs is of peculiar fineness, and would make rich garments. Hence the phrase of modern scholars, "gathering the fox hair from the ribs (choice Literary extracts) to make robes." There is no trace of demon foxes in the early records.

"The present idea about foxes seem to be of later growth. But in the oldest dictionary of China, it is stated that the fox is the courser upon which ghostly beings ride (as the Immortals on the backs of cranes). Nowadays they are regarded as mischievous fairies. They can make the seals of higher mandarins disappear. My grandfather, though not a mandarin, thought this might account for his own seal's disappearance, until he found that two men were missing. So the Viceroy, when he comes into office, does his best to propitiate the fairy foxes; and in the north, rich men have a 'fox chamber,' wherein victuals are daily provided.

"The suspicious nature of the fox is proved by its listening to the sound of the ice under its feet when he crosses it."

"But they are artful!" interjected one of the listeners.

"Yes; there is a fable spoken to a king of old time by one of his ministers. 'A she fox was overtaken by a tiger, which was about to devour her. The fox remonstrated with the tiger, and claimed that she possessed a superiority over other animals, all of whom she declared stood in awe of her. In proof of this, she invited the tiger to accompany her, and witness her power.

The tiger consented, and quietly followed. Every beast fled at their approach, and the tiger dare not attack the fox, not considering that the terror was caused by his own appearance. Thereafter, when the fox was seen in public, the other animals suspected that the tiger—with whom she seemed to be on such intimate terms—was at her heels. Hence the saying, "The fox arrogating the tiger's power to terrify." ' "

"It is the female fox that has the greatest power of transformation, I have heard," said Li Fing. Our Scholar's brother-in-law told me of the case of a countryman who lived near his home. He was very poor, and lived in a mud-brick hut with thatched roof. Having no wife he was wont to cook one meal a day, and eat the cold leavings in the morning. A fox took pity upon him, and, when he was out, entered the house, changed himself into a woman, cleaned up the place, cooked a meal for him, and then disappeared. This went on for some days until the farmer determined to watch and find out who his kind and unknown visitor was. So he crouched behind a water jar and waited. Soon he observed a fox entering through a hole in the wall, then turn a somersault, landing on her feet a handsome woman, the fox's skin falling to the ground. The farmer got hold of the skin, and secreted it under the pig's trough. When all her good deeds were done, she came and searched, but, not finding the skin, had to remain a woman, and became the farmer's wife. In after years he said jokingly to one of his children, 'Your mother is a fox.' The mother asked for his proof of such a statement. He produced the fox skin, when, turning a somersault, his wife entered the skin and run off, never to return again. Yes as I said, it is the female fox that has the power of transformation, is it not, Kno Tzu Chien?"

But before Kno Tzu Chien could reply, another said, "Undoubtedly it is. There was once a tailor living a hundred li from,—I forget where, —who had a fairy fox for a wife. No one else saw her but himself. But she taught him about all sorts of medicinal herbs, and he was looked upon as a great doctor."

"Well," said Kno Tzu Chien, "the book of Odes does say that the male fox is solitary and suspicious."

"There, I said so!" cried Li triumphantly.

"But the male fox is also credited with transforming powers," added Kno Tzu Chien ,"as the following story will show: The scholarly son of a high military official, having himself come into a mandarinship, went one evening to study in a hitherto disused chamber. The door was shut close, but from a crack in the window there entered a thin form, which, having rubbed its body for a while, filled out into a man's shape. The strange visitor advanced with a bow, and described himself as a reynard Immortal who had occupied that room for a hundred years, the former mandarins permitting him to do so. 'But as you have come here, I cannot stand in the way of an Imperial statesman; and so have come to explain that if you must study here, I will give way, if I may be allowed three days' grace. But perhaps you will be compassionate, and have the door closed as before.' The mandarin laughed, saying, 'There are scholars then among the foxes?' 'There are examinations for foxes held every year by the Lady of the Tai San (a hill in West Shantung),' replied the fox, 'where degrees are given to those worthy of them; the rest are regarded as wild foxes, and are not, like the others, allowed to compete for the rank of immortals. If I may exhort you, it seems sad that honourable men do not seek after that state. It is so much harder for us; we have first to learn to change into men's shape, then study their speech; in order to which latter, we have to learn

the cries of all the birds within the four seas and
nine continents.   Altogether it takes us five
hundred years, whereas men are spared this first
five hundred years' painstaking.   Honourable
and Literary men, moreover, have a further advantage over ordinary mortals of three hundred
years, and as a rule can give the desired rank of
immortals in a thousand years.'   The Mandarin,
accepting this explanation, retired from that
chamber.   In after years he used to tell his son
that his only regret was that he had not inquired
into the topics set by the Lady of the Tai San."

At this stage, more tea was handed around,
real tea brought by Kno Tzu Chien from Han-
Yang, which, when brewed into a pale golden
liquid, was the more fragrant and palatable owing to the presence of Jasmine flowers which
floated on the top.

The conversation therefore turned on the subject of tea.

THE ORIGIN OF TEA
Told By
KNO TZU CHIEN

"The 'Military Emperor' of the Sui dynasty (R. 589-605) was once afflicted with bad dreams, in which a spirit seemed to move his brain bones about until his head ached frightfully. He met a Buddhist monk, however, who told him that on the mountains grew a certain plant called O'ha which would heal him. The Emperor followed his advice with complete success. From that time on the beneficial effects of tea became known the wide Empire over."

The village "doctor," who is one of the company, feels that his province has been invaded. He has heard the true and authentic history of the discovery of the tea plant. "There was a man in ancient times," he would beg to repeat, "who was lying down in the forest 'on the occasion of' his dying, 'on the occasion of' his having been bitten by a large centipede. He lay almost helpless, but 'on the occasion of' his seeing a bush near, and being dry in the mouth, began to chew the leaves. 'On the occasion of' his doing so he revived, and (doubtless on all possible occasions) recommended the plant to all his friends. And what was that plant? It was tea. Ancient times! Sick man! Very sick! 'On the occasion of' his chewing! Quite well! Origin of tea—drinking!" And he burned his nose in the inclined cup of medicine, and looked out over the rim to see at a glance that Kno Tzu Chien was not convinced and that he had lost rather than gained position by his true and authentic contradiction of what the living encyclopædia said.

"There is indeed another account of the origin of tea," said Kno, "according to the Buddhists. There was a monk named Ta Ma (Darma, the third son of Kasiuwo, an Indian King) who came from the West to China (about 519 A.D.) to 'enlighten the Chinese.' He exposed himself to every possible hardship, being self-denying in the extreme.

This monk, lived only upon the herbs of the field; and, in order to attain to the highest degree of sanctity, determined to pass his nights as well as days in contemplation of doctrine. After some time spent thus, he became so weary that he fell asleep. This lapse troubled him sorely. He did not consider that his denying the five relations of sovereign and statesman, father and son, elder and younger brother, husband and wife, friend and companion, was at all contrary to the doctrine. Though this was the main point in the Memorial of Han Wen Nung against Buddhism.

"On awaking the next morning he determined to expiate his vow-breaking sin by cutting off his eyelids! Returning to the place the following day, he was surprised to find that each eyelid had become a shrub,—the plant, indeed, which we now call tea. He took of the leaves and ate them, and found as he did so his heart was filled with extraordinary exhilarations, and that he had acquired renewed strength for his contemplations. The event being known, his disciples spread the news far and wide."

The reader is hereby warned that the subject of the "soft, sober, sage, and venerable liquid; . . . smile-smoothing, heart-opening, wink-tipping cordial" (for thus a now forgotten poet-laureate of past days described it) is not yet finished; but while lips are smacking over the wonderful decoction of real tea (with none of your willow-leaf adulteration) we may peep into the minds of the hearers and note how perfectly harmonious these differing accounts seemed. Our flagstaff (as indispensable to us as a banner to a Chinese soldier) is now held in place by two main cords and a bit of hemp twine. It is so and so, it is such and such, it is otherwise, give a net result of perfect reliability. The audience is therefore sipping down indubitable truths with the tea.

Facts having been established in a most orthodox, three-ply manner, we are now prepared for poetic decorations. The Eastern mind scorns the merely matter-of-fact. But Kno Tzu Chien has begun to relate that "in the days of the first Emperor of the Eastern Ts'in dynasty (317–323) an old woman appeared in the streets with a vessel of fine tea in her hand, the contents of which she sold from morning until evening, for the vessel was inexhaustible. The proceeds of such sales she distributed among beggars and the indigent poor generally. But certain folks seized the old lady with the magic teapot and put her in jail. That night, however, both lady and teapot flew out the window."

"It was the Goddess of Mercy herself!" exclaimed Mrs. Li.

"It must have been!" said everybody else. After which Li protested that they had no right to cause their honored Kno Tzu Chien to split his throat with talking, but that if he had "two words" more on the subject, they would all "humbly receive his admonition."

He had just "two words." The first referred to the saying of an old monk, that old and new tea when mixed gave a harmonious but varied taste to the palate. There was a saying about the harpsichord, to the effect that the full resonance of the word was not evident until after a hundred years. It then gave all the delicate gradations answering to the phenomena of clearness and turbidity, of rain and sunshine, of heat and cold, which principle applied to tea also.

The second word was a comparison between the national beverage and the scholar's ink. "Tea-drinkers like a light-coloured decoction, and dislike a dark-coloured liquid. But it is quite otherwise with ink. Ink loses some of its brilliancy on being left in the slab overnight; tea leaves exposed for a day lose some of their scent. In this they resemble one another. New tea is most esteemed, but the more ancient the ink, the more excellent. In this they contrast. Tea for the mouth, and ink for the eye; but in old time there was a man of note who had a chronic complaint which forbade his drinking tea, yet had it brewed to please the eye. And another man

there was, who, though he could not write, was
fond of collecting good ink, which he would rub
and test by tasting—'a joke indeed for all who
hear it,' as my old book says." By way of post-
script, Kno added that a certain man of the Táng
dynasty, after drinking seven bowls of tea, experienced a stirring of air under the armpits, and
felt like flying to heaven.

THE MERCHANT'S SON

Told by

CHANG TI

In the province of Hunan there dwelt a man
who was engaged in trading abroad; and his
wife, who lived alone, dreamt one night that some
one was in her room. Waking up, she looked
about, and discovered a small creature which on
examination she knew to be a fox; but in a moment the thing had disappeared, although the
door had not been opened. The next evening
she asked the cook-maid to come and keep her
company; as also her own son, a boy of ten, who
was accustomed to sleep elsewhere. Towards
the middle of the night, when the cook and the
boy were fast asleep, back came the fox; and the

cook was waked up by hearing her mistress
muttering something as if she had nightmare.
The former then called out, and the fox ran
away; but from that moment the trader's wife
was not quite herself. When night came she
dared not blow out the candle, and bade her son
be sure and not sleep too soundly. Later on,
her son and the old woman having taken a nap
as they leant against the wall, suddenly waked
up and found her gone. They waited some time,
but she did not return, and the cook was too
frightened to go and look after her; so her son
took a light, and at length found her fast asleep
in another room. She didn't seem aware that
any thing particular had happened, but she became queerer and queerer every day, and
wouldn't have either her son or the cook to keep
her company any more. Her son, however,
made a point of running at once to his mother's
room if he heard any unusual sounds; and
though his mother always abused him for his
pains, he paid no attention to what she said.
Consequently, everyone thought him very brave,
though at the same time he was always indulging
in childish tricks. One day he played at being a
mason, and piled up stones upon the window-sill,
in spite of all that was said to him, and if any-

one took away a stone, he threw himself on the
ground, and cried like a child, so that nobody
dared go near him. In a few days he had got
both windows blocked up and the light excluded;
and then he set to filling up the chinks with
mud. He worked hard all day without mind-
ing the trouble, and when it was finished he
took and sharpened the kitchen chopper.
Everyone who saw him was disgusted with such
antics, and would take no notice of him. At
night he darkened his lamp, and, with the knife
concealed on his person, sat waiting for his
mother to mutter. As soon as she began he un-
covered his light, and, blocking up the doorway,
shouted out at the top of his voice. Nothing,
however, happened, and he moved from the door
a little way, when suddenly out rushed something like a fox, which was disappearing through
the door when he made a quick movement and
cut off about two inches of its tail, from which
the warm blood was still dripping as he brought
the light to bear upon it. His mother hereupon
cursed and reviled him, but he pretended not to
hear her, regretting only as he went to bed that
he hadn't hit the brute fair. But he consoled
himself by thinking that although he hadn't
killed it outright, he had done enough to prevent

its coming again. On the morrow he followed the tracks of blood over the wall and into the garden of a family named Ho; and that night, to his great joy, the fox did not reappear. His mother was meanwhile prostrate, with hardly any life in her, and in the midst of it all his father came home. The boy told him what had happened, at which he was much alarmed, and sent for a doctor to attend to his wife; but she only threw the medicine away, and cursed and swore horribly. So they secretly mixed the medicine with her tea and soup, and in a few days she began to get better, to the inexpressible delight of both her husband and son. One night, however, her husband woke up and found her gone; and after searching for her with the aid of his son, they discovered her sleeping in another room. From that time she became more eccentric than ever, and was always being found in strange places, cursing those who tried to remove her. Her husband was at his wits' end. It was of no use keeping the door locked, for it opened of itself at her approach; and he had called in any number of magicians to exorcise the fox, but without obtaining the slightest result, One evening her son concealed himself in the Ho family garden, and lay down in the long grass with a view to detecting the fox's retreat. As the moon rose he heard the sound of voices, and, pushing aside the grass, saw two people drinking, with a long-bearded servant pouring out their wine, dressed in an old dark-brown coat. They were whispering together, and he could not make out what they said; but by-and-by he heard one of them remark, "Get some white wine for to-morrow," and then they went away, leaving the long-bearded servant alone. The latter then threw off his coat, and lay down to sleep on the stones; whereupon the trader's son eyed him carefully, and saw that he was like a man in every respect except that he had a tail. The boy would then have gone home; but he was afraid the fox might hear him, and accordingly remained where he was till near dawn, when he saw the other two come back, one at a time, and then they all disappeared among the bushes. On reaching home his father asked him where he had been, and he replied that he had stopped the night with the Ho family. He then accompanied his father to the town, where he saw hanging up at a hat-shop a fox's tail, and finally, after much coaxing, succeeded in making his father buy it for him. While the latter was engaged in a shop, his son, who was playing about beside him, availed himself of a moment when his father was not looking and stole some money from him, and went off and bought a quantity of white wine, which he left in charge of the wine-merchant. Now an uncle of his, who was a sportsman by trade, lived in the city, and thither he next betook himself. His uncle was out, but his aunt was there, and inquired after the health of his mother. "She has been better the last few days," replied he; "but she is now very much upset by a rat having gnawed a dress of hers, and has sent me to ask for some poison." His aunt opened the cupboard and gave him about the tenth of an ounce in a piece of paper, which he thought was very little; so, when his aunt had gone to get him something to eat, he took the opportunity of being alone, opened the packet, and abstracted a large handful. Hiding this in his coat, he ran to tell his aunt that she needn't prepare anything for him, as his father was waiting in the market, and he couldn't stop to eat it. He then went off; and having quietly dropped the poison into the wine he had bought, went sauntering about the town. At nightfall he re- turned home, and told his father that he had been at his uncle's. This he continued to do for some time, until one day he saw among the crowd his long-bearded friend. Marking him closely, he followed him, and at length entered into conversation, asking him where he lived. "I live at Pei-ts'un," said he; "where do you live?" "I," replied the trader's son, falsely, "live in a hole on the hillside." The long-bearded man was considerably startled at his answer, but much more so when he added, "We've lived there for generations: haven't *you?*" The other man asked his name, to which the boy replied, "My name is Hu. I saw you with two gentlemen in the Ho family garden, and haven't forgotten you." Questioning him more fully, the long-bearded man was still in a half-and-half state of belief and doubt, when the trader's son opened his coat a little bit, and showed him the end of the tail he had bought, saying, "The like of us can mix with ordinary people, but unfortunately we can never get rid of this." The long-bearded man then asked him what he was doing there, to which he answered that his father had sent him to buy wine; thereupon the former remarked that that was exactly what he had come for, and the boy then inquired if he had bought it yet or not. "We are poor," replied the stranger, "and as a rule I prefer to steal it." "A difficult and dangerous job," observed the boy. "I have my master's instructions to get some," said the other, "and what am I to do?" The boy then asked him who his masters were, to which he replied that they were the two brothers the boy had seen that night. "One of them has bewitched a lady named Wang; and the other, the wife of a trader who lives near. The son of the last-mentioned lady is a violent fellow, and cut off my master's tail, so that he was laid up for ten days. But he is putting her under spells again now." He was then going away, saying he should never get his wine; but the boy said to him, "It's much easier to buy than steal. I have some at the wine-shop there which I will give to you. My purse isn't empty, and I can buy some more." The long-bearded man hardly knew how to thank him; but the boy said, "We're all one family. Don't mention such a trifle. When I have time I'll come and take a drink with you." So they went off together to the wine-shop, where the boy gave him the wine, and they then separated. That night his mother slept quietly and had no fits, and the boy knew that something must have happened. He then told his father, and they went to see if there were any results; when lo! they found both foxes stretched out dead in the arbour. One of the foxes was lying on the grass,

and out of its mouth blood was still trickling.
The wine-bottle was there; and on shaking it they
heard that some was left. Then his father
asked him why he had kept it all so secret; to
which the boy replied that foxes were very saga-
cious, and would have been sure to scent the plot.
Thereupon his father was mightily pleased, and
said he was a perfect sage for cunning. They
then carried the foxes home, and saw on the tail
of one of them the scar of a knife-wound. From
that time they were left in peace; but the trader's
wife became very thin, and though her reason returned, shortly afterwards died of consumption.
The other lady, Mrs. Wang, began to get better
as soon as the foxes had been killed; and as to
the boy, he was taught riding and archery by
his proud parent, and subsequently rose to high
rank in the army.

THE STONE FROM HEAVEN

Told by

WANG MANG

In Peking there lived a man named Hsing
Yün-fei, who was an amateur mineralogist and
would pay any price for a good specimen. One

day as he was fishing in the river, something caught his net, and diving down he brought up a stone about a foot in diameter, beautifully carved on all sides to resemble clustering hills and peaks. He was quite as pleased with this as if he had found some precious stone; and having had an elegant sandal-wood stand made for it, he set his prize upon the table. Whenever it was about to rain, clouds, which from a distance looked like new cotton-wool, would come forth from each of the holes or grottoes on the stone, and appear to close them up. By-and-by an influential personage called at the house and begged to see the stone, immediately seizing it and handing it over to a lusty servant, at the same time whipping his horse and riding away. Hsing was in despair; but all he could do was to mourn the loss of the stone, and indulge his anger against the thief. Meanwhile, the servant, who had carried off the stone on his back, stopped to rest at a bridge; when all of a sudden his hand slipped and the stone fell into the water. His master was extremely put out at this, and gave him a sound beating; subsequently hiring several divers, who tried every means in their power to recover the stone, but were quite unable to find it. He then went away, having first published a notice of reward, and by these means many were tempted to seek for the stone.   Soon after, Hsing himself came to the spot, and as he mournfully approached the bank, lo! the water became clear, and he could see the stone lying at the bottom.   Taking off his clothes, he quickly jumped in and brought it out, together with the sandalwood stand, which was still with it.   He carried it off home, and being no longer desirous of showing it to people, he had an inner room cleaned and put it there.   Some time afterwards an old man knocked at the door and asked to be allowed to see the stone; whereupon Hsing replied that he had lost it a long time ago. "Isn't that it in the inner room?" said the old man smiling.   "Oh, walk in and see for yourself if you don't believe me," answered Hsing; and the old man did walk in, and there was the stone on the table.   This took Hsing very much aback; and the old man then laid his hand upon the stone and said, "This is an old family relic of mine: I lost it many months since.   How does it come to be here?   I pray you now restore it to me."   Hsing didn't know what to say, but declared he was the owner of the stone; upon which the old man remarked, "If it is really yours, what evidence can you bring to prove it?"

Hsing made no reply; and the old man continued, "To show you that I know this stone, may mention that it has altogether ninety-two grottoes, and that in the largest of these are five words:

"A stone from Heaven above."

Hsing looked and found that there·were actually some small characters, no larger than grains of rice, which by straining his eyes a little he managed to read; also, that the number of grottoes was as the old man had said. However, he would not give him the stone; and the old man laughed, and asked, "Pray what right have you to keep other people's things?" He then bowed and went away, Hsing escorting him as far as the door; but when he returned to the room, the stone had disappeared. In a great fright, he ran after the old man, who had walked slowly and was not far off, and seizing his sleeve entreated him to give back the stone. "Do you think," said the latter, "that I could conceal a stone a foot in diameter in my sleeve?" But Hsing knew that he must be superhuman, and led him back to the house, where he threw himself on his knees and begged that ·he might have the stone. "Is it yours or mine?" asked the old man. "Of course it is yours," replied Hsing, "though

I hope you will consent to deny yourself the pleasure of keeping it." "In that case," said the old man, "it is back again"; and going into the inner room, they found the stone in its old place. "The jewels of this world," observed Hsing's visitor, "should be given to those who know how to take care of them. This stone can choose its own master, and I am very pleased that it should remain with you; at the same time I must inform you that it was in too great a hurry to come into the world of mortals, and has not yet been freed from all contingent calamities. I had better take it away with me, and three years hence you shall have it again. If, however you insist on keeping it, then your span of life will be shortened by three years, that your terms of existence may harmonise together. Are you willing?" Hsing said he was; whereupon the old man with his fingers closed up three of the stone's grottoes, which yielded to his touch like mud. When this was done, he turned to Hsing and told him that the grottoes on that stone represented the years of his life; and then he took his leave, firmly refusing to remain any longer, and not disclosing his name.

More than a year after this, Hsing had occasion to go away on business, and in the night a thief broke in and carried off the stone, taking nothing else at all. When Hsing came home, he was dreadfully grieved, as if his whole object in life was gone; and made all possible inquiries and efforts to get it back, but without the slightest result. Some time passed away, when one day going into a temple Hsing noticed a man selling stones, and amongst the rest he saw his old friend. Of course he immediately wanted to regain possession of it; but as the stone-seller would not consent, he shouldered the stone and went off to the nearest mandarin. The stone-seller was then asked what proof he could give that the stone was his; and he replied that the number of the grottoes was eighty-nine. Hsing inquired if that was all he had to say, and when the other acknowledged that it was, he himself told the magistrate what were the characters inscribed within, also calling attention to the finger marks at the closed-up grottoes. He therefore gained his case, and the mandarin would have bambooed the stone-seller, had he not declared that he bought it in the market for twenty ounces of silver,—whereupon he was dismissed.

A high official next offered Hsing one hundred ounces of silver for it; but he refused to sell it even for ten thousand, which so enraged the would-be purchaser that he worked up a case against Hsing, and got him put in prison. Hsing was thereby compelled to pawn a great deal of his property; and then the official sent some one to try if the affair could not be managed through his son, to which Hsing, on hearing of the attempt, steadily refused to consent, saying that he and the stone could not be parted even in death. His wife, however, and his son, laid their heads together and sent the stone to the high official, and Hsing only heard of it when he arrived home from the prison. He cursed his wife and beat his son, and frequently tried to make away with himself, though luckily his servants always managed to prevent him from succeeding. At night he dreamt that a noble-looking personage appeared to him and said, "My name is Shih Ch'ing-hsü—(Stone from Heaven). Do not grieve. I purposely quitted you for a year and more; but next year on the 20th of the eighth moon, at dawn, come to the Hai-tai Gate and buy me back for two strings of cash." Hsing was overjoyed at this dream, and carefully took down the day mentioned. Meanwhile the stone was at the official's private house; but as the cloud manifestations ceased, the stone was less and less prized; and the following year when the official was disgraced for maladministration and subsequently died, Hsing met some of his servants at the Hai-tai Gate going off to sell the stone, and purchased it back from them for two strings of cash.

Hsing lived till he was eighty-nine; and then having prepared the necessaries for his interment, bade his son bury the stone with him, which was accordingly done.   Six months later robbers broke into the vault and made off with the stone, and his son tried in vain to secure their capture; however, a few days afterwards, he was travelling with his servants, when suddenly two men rushed forth dripping with perspiration, and looking up into the air, acknowledged their crime, saying, "Mr. Hsing, please don't torment us thus!   We took the stone and sold it for only four ounces of silver."   Hsing's son and his servants then seized these men, and took them before the magistrate, where they at once acknowledged their guilt.   Asking what had become of the stone, they said they had sold it to a member of the magistrate's family; and when it was produced, that official took such a fancy to it that he gave it to one of his servants and bade him place it in the treasury.   Thereupon the stone slipped out of the servant's hand and broke into a hundred pieces, to the great astonishment of all present. The magistrate now had the thieves bambooed and sent them away; but Hsing's son picked up the broken pieces of the stone, and buried them in his father's grave.

THE THUNDER GOD

Told by

KEY FAH

Yo Yün-Hao and Hsia P'ing-tzŭ lived as boys in the same village, and when they grew up read with the same tutor, becoming the firmest of friends. Hsia was a clever fellow, and had acquired some reputation even at the early age of ten. Yo was not a bit envious, but rather looked up to him, and Hsia in return helped his friend very much with his studies, so that he, too, made considerable progress. This increased Hsia's fame, though try as he would he could never succeed at the public examinations, and by-and-by he sickened and died. His family was so poor they could not find money for his burial, whereupon Yo came forward and paid all expenses, besides taking care of his widow and children.

Every peck or bushel he would share with them, the widow trusting entirely to his support;

and thus he acquired a good name in the village, though not being a rich man himself, he soon ran through all his own property. "Alas!" cried he, "where talents like Hsia's failed, can I expect to succeed? Wealth and rank are matters of destiny, and my present career will only end by my dying like a dog in a ditch. I must try something else." So he gave up book-learning and went into trade, and in six months he had a trifle of money in hand.

One day when he was resting at an inn in Nanking, he saw a great big fellow walk in and seat himself at no great distance in a very melancholy mood. Yo asked him if he was hungry, and on receiving no answer, pushed some food over towards him. The stranger immediately set to feeding himself by handfuls, and in no time the whole had disappeared. Yo ordered another supply, but that was quickly disposed of in like manner; and then he told the landlord to bring a shoulder of pork and a quantity of boiled dumplings. Thus, after eating enough for half a dozen, his appetite was appeased and he turned to thank his benefactor, saying, "For three years I haven't had such a meal." "And why should a fine fellow like you be in such a state of destitution?" inquired Yo; to which the other only replied, "The judgments of heaven may not be discussed." Being asked where he lived, the stranger replied, "On land I have no home, on the water no boat; at dawn in the village, at night in the city." Yo then prepared to depart; but his friend would not leave him, declaring that he was in imminent danger, and that he could not forget the late kindness Yo had shown him. So they went along together, and on the way Yo invited the other to eat with him; but this he refused, saying that he only took food occasionally. Yo marvelled more than ever at this; and next day when they were on the river a great storm arose and capsized all their boats, Yo himself being thrown into the water with the others. Suddenly the gale abated and the stranger bore Yo on his back to another boat, plunging at once into the water and bringing back the lost vessel, upon which he placed Yo and bade him remain quietly there. He then returned once more, this time carrying in his arms a part of the cargo, which he replaced in the vessel, and so he went on until it was all restored. Yo thanked him, saying, "It was enough to save my life; but you have added to this the restoration of my goods." Nothing, in fact, had been lost, and now Yo began to regard the stranger as something more than

human.   The latter here wished to take his leave,
but Yo pressed him so much to stay that at last
he consented to remain.   Then Yo remarked
that after all he had lost a gold pin, and immediately the stranger plunged into the water again,
rising at length to the surface with the missing
article in his mouth, and presenting it to Yo with
the remark that he was delighted to be able to
fulfill his commands.   The people on the river
were all much astonished at what they saw;
meanwhile Yo went home with his friend, and
there they lived together, the big man only eating once in ten or twelve days, but then display-
ing an enormous appetite.   One day he spoke of
going away, to which Yo would by no means
consent; and as it was just then about to rain and
thunder, he asked him to tell him what the clouds
were like, and what thunder was, also how he
could get up to the sky and have a look, so as to
set his mind at rest on the subject.   "Would you
like to have a ramble among the clouds?" asked
the stranger, as Yo was lying down to take a
nap; on awaking from which he felt himself spin-
ning along through the air, and not at all as if he
were lying on a bed.   Opening his eyes he saw he
was among the clouds, and around him was a
fleecy atmosphere.   Jumping up in great alarm,

he felt giddy as if he had been at sea, and underneath his feet he found a soft, yielding substance unlike the earth. Above him were the stars, and this made him think he was dreaming; but looking up he saw that they were set in the sky like seeds in the cup of a lily, varying from the size of the biggest bowl to that of a small basin. On raising his hand he discovered that the large stars were all tightly fixed; but he managed to pick a small one, which he concealed in his sleeve; and then parting the clouds beneath him, he looked through and saw the sea glittering like silver below. Large cities appeared no bigger than beans—just at this moment, however, he bethought himself that if his foot were to slip, what a tremendous fall he would have. He now beheld two dragons writhing their way along, and drawing a cart with a huge vat in it, each movement of their tails sounding like the crack of a bullock-driver's whip. The vat was full of water and numbers of men were employed in ladling it out and sprinkling it on the clouds. These men were astonished at seeing Yo; however, a big fellow among them called out, "All right, he's my friend," and then they gave him a ladle to help them throw the water out. Now it happened to be a very dry season, and when Yo got hold of the ladle he took good care to throw the water so that it should all fall on and around his own home. The stranger then told him that he was an assistant to the God of Thunder, and that he had just returned from a three years' punishment inflicted on him in consequence of some neglect of his in the matter of rain. He added that they must now part; and taking the long rope which had been used as reins for the cart, bade Yo grip it tightly, that he might be let down to earth. Yo was afraid of this, but on being told there was no danger he did so, and in a moment whish-h-h-h-h—away he went and found himself safe and sound on *terra firma*. He discovered that he had descended outside his native village, and then the rope was drawn up into the clouds and he saw it no more. The drought had been excessive; for three or four miles round very little rain had fallen, though in Yo's own village the water-courses were all full. On reaching home he took the star out of his sleeve, and put it on the table. It was dull-looking like an ordinary stone; but at night it became very brilliant and lighted up the whole house. This made him value it highly, and he stored it carefully away, bringing it out only when he had guests, to light them at their wine.

It was always thus dazzling bright, until one evening when his wife was sitting with him doing her hair, the star began to diminish in brilliancy, and to flit about like a fire-fly. Mrs. Yo sat gaping with astonishment, when all of a sudden it flitted into her mouth and ran down her throat. She tried to cough it up, but couldn't, to the very great amazement of her husband. That night Yo dreamt that his old friend Hsia appeared before him and said, "I am the Shao-wei star. Your friendship is still cherished by me, and now you have brought me back from the sky. Truly our destinies are knitted together and I will repay your kindness by becoming your son." Now Yo was thirty years of age, but without sons; however, after this dream his wife bore him a male child, and they called his name Star. He was extraordinarily clever, and at sixteen years of age took his master's degree.

YANG SUNG'S DREAM

It had been a merry evening on Yang Sung's boat. A little disagreement in the early evening had been settled by Yang Sung's good humor, the locator going on shore to secure a supply of wine, which having cost him nothing, he the more freely distributed. The lieutenant was on shore, as also the semi-officials of the other boats, who had found the days of Tsaitien long and the nights insipid. So the rest had a merry time. Yang Sung, though not an abstainer, was rallied on his meager abilities at imbibing. In polite circles there is quite a gamut of compliments in use on the subject of a man's ability to drink wine, and a corresponding gamut of humble disclaimers. No such compliments fell to the lot of the sturdy lad of eighteen and a half, but he could tell a tale or two by this time.

It was the fourth watch before there was anything like quiet, and then the shouts were but exchanged for thunderous snores. Yang Sung, being still sober, was to watch for the remainder of the night. The custom was for two men to divide the night watch between them. His boat being the chief one in the little fleet, it fell to his lot when he heard the drum beats from the central station to take up the two sticks, and pass the sound on to those higher up the river, to the night watchman, and the wakeful public generally. Having done so, he felt very sleepy. He must lie down. Everything was still, but a lamp here and there flickering in the high wind, and the cry of "Blood, blood" (pig's blood), which sounded well-nigh demoniacal,—what customers do these night hawkers get?—proclaimed that there was a busy town near, with its more than half a million inhabitants. The lantern on the bows all but blotted out the outline of the houses. He would read until daylight. The volume he picked was of the "Making of the Gods," which he used to read to the lieutenant. The Taoist's description of heaven was now familiar, and the various poems and descriptive pieces he was learning by heart. The piece for tonight was the description of a fire, in which a sprite was exposed and consumed. It seemed too fine for the occasion, but poets are wont to deal in hyperbole. "Dense smoke encaged, dense smoke encaged the corner-stones of earth," he repeated to himself several times, until he was interrupted by a shout, then another. Something was happening on shore. He tried to arouse the sleepers. They but swore, and turned over, snoring again. But the shouts increased. Then a light appeared far away to the right hand. It seemed to spread toward the centre. A man ran along the bank, crying, "Demons!" He was a night watchman, only proof against distant thieves.

"Stand!" shouted Yang Sung. "What is it?"

"Demons with torches. Hundreds of them!"
cried the man, and ran on.

The glare became unmistakable; more fugitives with the same tale; more efforts on the lad's
part to waken the sleepers, until, the shouts on
shore increasing, he took up his drumstick and
belaboured the hands of one or two. He was
cursed, he was seized. Everyone seemed to
strike out at once. "Demons!" he shouted amid
his struggles; then he changed to "The Pirates
are upon us."

At this familiar cry some began to rouse themselves and yawn. They let him go. He seized
a petard or two, and fired it outside. General
cry of muffled voices. "What is it?" More
shouts on shore, and the glare, which had now
reached the spot opposite to him; no, it extended
farther to the west. "Demons! Pirates! Fire!"
was shouted, was screamed, was yelled on shore.
"They are near. They have taken Wu Seng
Miao. I heard their guns. Run!"

It was not glare now, it was flame. Huge
tongues of flame shot up above the houses, light-
ing up the figures of men and women bold enough
to go up for a moment on to the wooden lofts
above the roofs. The upper story of Wu Seng
Miao gateway, where only an old Vegetarian's

tiny lamp is to be seen as a rule, was full of fire-lit faces. Luminous smoke rolled overhead, carried by the high wind afar. It rained sparks. The heat was unbearable. The summer's night was becoming hot as an oven.

A splash! It was a man leaping on to a boat: no, ten men had made the leap, one had fallen. His body was whirled on by the rapid current. His cries were unheard in the general roar. Down the steep bank came men, women, and children, bearers of boxes and bundles and babies; they fell in a heap on the boats or into the water. The bows were nearly sinking. "Quick, unloose the chains! Let the grappling irons go. Clear the way, all of you," and a dozen were pushed into the water, to cling upon the boat-sides until they dropped, carried down with the rest. The river was thick with bodies. "Bring a hatchet." The chain will not be undone. Hew away at the block which holds it. Harder! Faster! See that great mass of humanity tumbling down the bank. Only just in time. They would have swamped us. It is light as day. To the oars, every one of you; shake off the clinging hands. Off! Across the river. Push this boat and that with your hooks, never mind the men who cling there. Curse and rave, but push—

row! The river is half-blocked. See a boat has
overturned! Look at that mass of boats above!
The river is narrowed here. There will be a fa-
tal block in a moment. Row for your lives!
Blocked it is, but we are in the front. Look
out! That great salt junk is overturning. Out
of the way of the mast. Our comrades' boat is
snapped in two. There are demons in the current. The oars bend, they break. Use your
poles and broken oars. We must get across.
Hands off. We must live. Splash, splash!
Shrieks! Curses! But we have reached the
other side. "Save life, save life!" Who can
save a hundred? The cries are lost in the roar
of the fire, the crackling of slates, and the terrific yells of ten thousand in death agonies. The
kingdom of hell has come. It is pandemonium
on earth.

To stay there on the boat is to be scorched.
There is no commander to give orders, so it is
every man for himself. Struggle for dear life.
See the boats have caught. Clamber up the
banks as the others do. They fall, dragged down
by clinging hands. Over the shifting mass.
Up again. The water has but cooled you.
There is a blank space. Press in. Just in time.

On dry land with a chance for life if you out-run the thick rain of sparks.

The path led from a small temple to the god of boatmen,—already on fire,—to— the "Ancient Bell Tower," on the "Moon Lake Causeway." It was well for Yang Sung that he had a bit of tolerably clear road, for the latter path was one mass of fugitives, unable to proceed by reason of a block by the bell-tower archway.   In a densely crowded road, an archway narrowing it by one-half may stop all progress.   The crowd forms one compact mass too wide for the gateway.

Happily, the youth was on the outside, and could go round, wading through a swamp on the left.   On the right, many were drowned in the lake.   But he must join the main path farther on, as part of the lake waters come through a bridge, and it is too deep to wade there.   But there was another dense crowd by the bridge, those on the outside being jammed against the granite posts and the connecting poles.   Among them was a man dressed in silks whose head was bleeding.   His voice was heard above the gen-eral din, shouting, "A thousand cash for a boat!" Then "Two thousand," then, finally, "An ingot of silver." But the boats had gone.   The pole gave way, and, with many others, he fell into the water.

Under one of the buttresses was a man with a boathook, with which he caught hold of the garments of the wealthy man, who, grasping his bundle, laid hold of the outstretched pole. The holder thereof seized the bundle, then calmly shook off the man, nay, pushed him under with the hook, and held him there. Was it a dream? The man's face seemed familiar. It looked like that of Lieu! Yang Sung now for the first time discovered that he had his musket with him. He had snatched it up mechanically as he sprang from the boat. He had loaded it at the first alarm. An irresistible impulse made him point it at the dark form under the bridge, but it was wet. Some folks from the archway came crowding up. It was hopeless for him to try and ascend where so many were being pushed over. One thing remained, he could wade round the bit of lake on the left. But, reaching drier ground, he stumbled, and swooned away.

A spark upon his cheek proved a speedy restorative, and he came to consciousness, to notice that Tortoise Hill was not far off. Limping along dry land, wading through swamp, he reached the foot of the Hill, with just enough energy left to clamber half-way up the rocky sides. Here he found two masses of rock which almost met at the top. Into this cavern-like recess he crawled, held his musket mechanically, and sat down. His head was bleeding, and he was very faint. The horrid glare before him seemed part of a hideous nightmare. But he was out of range of the sparks.

Before long, however, the ground seemed to shake. The rebels had taken the hill from the other side, had fired a volley which he felt rather than heard, and had struck his musket from his hand. Such was the dream which passed through his bewildered mind in an instant of time. His last moment had come! He had escaped the flames but to perish by a sword-thrust. His whole life rushed before him. Lieu and his son, the teacher and his wife, their marriage, his father and mother. He began to cry, "My mother! my mother!" But the dark mass before him had gone. It was not a band of Pirates. It was a large boulder loosened by the pressure of the crowd on the hill-top, which had come rolling down, falling full force upon the two pieces of rock under which he had been sitting. Poised there an instant, it had fallen upon his gun-barrel, and, crushing that, had gone crashing down toward the swamp far beneath. He realized what had happened now.

It was unlikely that another such boulder would follow suit, but the lad's nerves were shaken, and picking up his shattered musket with soldierly instinct, he clambered up higher. He could not be dreaming now. There were undoubted sounds of firing. If his ears deceived him, his eyes did not. There was a general stampede along the ridge of the hill. Getting nearer, he heard the cry, "Pirates! Pirates!"

The fugitives did not seem to be pursued, though the firing continued. He was unable to run, and seemed not to care now whether he died or not. He would scramble up to the top and see what had happened. He had to rest very frequently, and each time he sank to the ground there was that sight before him. It was as real when he tried to shut his eyes and turn away, as when he looked in that direction. Four miles of towering flame! The wooden-framed dwellings of six hundred thousand, among them those whom he had seen bustling along the crowded street under the gay sign-boards! That sharper, where was he? Where was the Taoist pedlar,—not his Taoist, whom he saw shot through the back when the imperialist came, but that

other Taoist? Well, it could not be helped.
But those busy shops with their shopmen and
customers? It could not be. He was in the
street again. No, he was alone near the hill-top
on that awfully sultry night. "Dense smoke encaged, encaged the corner-stones of earth."
Had the writer of the lines seen a city on fire?
Four miles of flame.

But he must struggle onto the top. When he
had done so, he found that the firing was from the
Hanyang walls. It was a cannonade. Yes,
there was a double row of yellow jackets returning the fire from behind earthworks below that
blazing mass a quarter of a mile off. What was
that mass? The temple, of course. Seven temples, he remembered. See, a shot aimed too high
has hit one of them, and carried off with it blazing beams and a firey shower of ignited stuff
down over the steep sides of the rock.

The scene at the end of the hill seemed to be
absorbed in the wider facts of that terrible night.
There is a point beyond which the already dazed
brain ceases to receive further shock, and he sat
looking on, like an overtired spectator at a thea-
tre. He seemed to be going off into a stupor.

Time passed unheeded. It might have been
half an hour, it might have been two hours, but

he realized by and by that the firing had ceased, and that there was a form before him, squatting down upon its heels, with an evil smile on its face.

"Hallo! you mandarin soldier, are you dead like the rest? Alive? Well, look yonder. A fine sight, is it not, better than a bonfire of paper houses?"

Was it a demon or a man? It was a young man. Its voice was unmistakable. It was Lieu Fah.

He raised himself, and pointed his musket at the figure. That was enough. It disappeared with a shriek. It crouched behind a gravestone, then ran, then crouched behind another, then ran again. Until half-way down the hill it was stopped by a man who raised himself from the ground. He had a yellow sleeveless jacket on, clearly discernible in the glare. He hurriedly took it off, and his under coat too, put it on again, and the blue jacket with sleeves over it. The younger of the two pointed with the finger up the hill–top. Yang Sung pointed his musket at them, and both ran off, bearing what seemed to be heavy burdens.

He was alone again. The glare seemed to increase, for the furthur horizon could not be defined. The temples were still blazing, and on

the left was that awful glare.   Whence came the
increasing light?   Look, over Wuchang yonder
there is a great ball of fire!   What new wonder
was that?   Then Yang Sung felt himself being
roughly shaken, and a familiar voice shouting
with each shake, "Wake up!   Wake up!   Yang
Sung.   You have slept on deck all night, and the
rising sun pouring its glorious rays in your face,
is the 'new wonder.'"   Yang Sung opened his
eyes, to behold Lieu Fah, calling him to view the
beauty of the dawn.   Was it the reading of
"The Making of the Gods" or the drinking of the
wine that caused Yang Sung's Dream?

KUNG PENG TAH AND THE WOODCUTTER

Told by

TUNG CHOU KION

"A tale I tell of wondrous sympathy,
For those alone that sympathetic be."

"In the old days described in the Spring and
Autumn Annals, when China consisted of a host
of rival States hard to amalgamate, there lived a
celebrated Statesman of the name of Kung Peng
Tah.   His birthplace was the capital of the kingdom of Ch'u, which is now the present Kingchow

(the 'island of thorn bushes' to which Ts'ao Ts'ao sent his cynical adviser Ti'ao Hen), to the west of the modern Wuchang. But his star of good fortune led him into an official post in the kingdom of T'sin, which occupied what is now the southern half of Shensi, and the north-west of Honan.

"The King of Tsin, wishing to send an embassy of friendly congratulation to the King of Ch'u, Kung Peng Tah sought and obtained the commission. Having reached the capital, he was granted a royal interview, and was entertained in sumptuous style. He naturally wished to visit his ancestral graves, and call upon such of his relatives and friends as the great change-worker Time had spared yet.

"Public business being ended, he took his leave of his royal host, pleading that he was suffering from ill-health, which would be aggravated by jolting over rough roads; and so provision was made for him to return by water, two boats being fitted up for his accommodation. The fact was, he wished to feast his eyes once more upon the familiar landscapes of ten or twenty years back. All the officials of the capital accompanied him to the river bank, so the parting was even more honourable than the reception had been.

KUNG PENG TAH AND THE WOODCUTTER

"The wind-filled sails advanced amid the thousand tiers of blue-green wavelets, while beyond the sunlit waters were the distant hills of piled-up turquoise. It was mid-autumn, and Kung Peng Tah enjoyed the varied scenery to the full.

"Passing Hanyang, the boats left the Yangtse; but either the Han had another channel then, or else it was flood time, for he seems to enter the chain of lakes which extend from Hanyang to beyond the Hill of the Nine Recluses.

Kung Peng Tah had not gone many miles before a fierce wind sprang up, and the rain poured in torrents, so that the boats had to make for the nearest bank, which happened to be not far from the 'Horse Saddle' Hill.

"After sundown the storm abated, and the full-orbed moon shone forth, all the brighter for the rain. Peng Tah being alone, with nothing to occupy his thoughts, ordered his boy to light the incense brazier and bring out his harpsichord. The sweet instrument (which sounds like a piano with both pedals down) being brought, the musician adjusted the strings, and commenced a plaintive strain. Before he had played many notes, however, one of the strings snapped with a loud noise. At this he was very much startled and told the lad to go outside and inquire what manner of place it was. The head boatman replied that it was a mere uncultivated hill, with no cottages in sight. 'A mere uncultivated hill?' the musician exclaimed. 'Had it been a city or village near which we were stopping, there might have been some scholar or other listening to my instrument, and thus causing the string to break. I have it! There is some villain or other near who owes me a grudge, or a robber bent on stealing the treasure in the boats. If he is not among the trees yonder, he is certainly hiding among the tall reeds.'

"The boatman went to look, when they heard a voice exclaim, 'The high official need not disturb himself; I do not belong to the robber class. I am a woodcutter caught in the storm, and so took refuge here. Then hearing the classical strains of the harpsichord, I stopped to listen.'

"'A likely tale,' laughed the statesman, 'a hillside woodcutter a musical connoisseur; and his attendants ordered the intruder off. But he remained expostulating, saying, 'The high official is wrong. Has he not heard that "in a village of ten houses there is sure to be found loyalty and truth?" And where there is a true gentleman, there will be gentlemanly visitors. If you, sir, make out that on a wild hill there are none capable of appreciating music, it may be argued that there will be no guest at the foot of such a hill playing at midnight.'

"Surprised to hear such a clever reply, Peng Tah went to the door, and said, half in sarcasm, 'As the gentleman upon the bank has been listening thus attentively, perhaps he will tell me what sort of a tune I was playing!'

" 'If I had not understood the meaning of the music, is it likely that I should remain listening? The poem you were expressing in musical notes was that in which Confucius bemoans the early death of his favorite disciple Yen Hwui. The words are these—

> "Alas, Yen Hwui, so soon to die!
> My hair with grief is turned to gray.
> Thy frugal joys, thy humble home,"—

at which point the string snapped. But the fourth line I remember to be—

> "Shall charm the ages yet to come." '

" 'You, sir, are no ordinary countryman!' exclaimed Peng Tah. 'The bank is too distant for conversation, will you not come nearer?' So he ordered the boatmen to throw out a plank and assist the scholar into the boat.

The attendants did so, and the young man

came on board—a veritable woodcutter, clad in straw cape and rain hat, grasping an iron-shod coolie pole; a hatchet was stuck in his girdle, and he had straw sandals on his feet! What did the underlings know about intelligent conversation? They saw a mere woodcutter. 'Be sure and knock your head on the ground in the presence of the official,' they said. 'And when he speaks to you be careful how you answer him. He is a high statesman.'

" 'Do not insult me,' was the reply. 'Wait till I have adjusted my apparel for the inter-view.' And he proceeded to divest himself of rain hat, to display a blue cloth wrapped round his head; then his grass cape, to display to view a cotton jacket, bound round with a white girdle, with drawers to match. Not a whit flurried, he placed his rain hat and grass cape, his spiked pole and hatchet, outside the door, took off his straw sandals, wrung the dirty water from them, put them on afresh, and entered.

"The statesman was sitting upon the divan, amid the brilliant glow of lamps and candles. Seeing whom, the woodcutter just made a deep bow, saying, 'I pay you my respects, sir.'

An official of Peng Tah's standing could

hardly be expected to give a common woodcutter a polite reception. But having invited him on board, he could hardly drive him away. He just waved his hand slightly, saying, 'No need for ceremony,' and called the lad to bring a seat. A long bench being brought, the official shouted out, 'Sit down.' The woodcutter, without any phrase of abject appreciation of the honour, took his seat with the utmost composure. At this Peng Tah was rather put out, and neither asked his name nor ordered the usual tea.

"They sat in awkward silence for a long time, till the official, in an irritated tone of voice, exclaimed, 'So you are the listener on the bank?' to which the woodcutter replied with the usual phrase, 'I do not presume!'

" 'Well, as you were listening, you doubtless know the origin of the instrument, who invented the harpsichord, and what good there is in playing it?'

" 'Receiving your question with all due deference, I may, however, delay the boat with my tedious replies!' For the boatman had just been to say there was nothing to prevent their starting.

" 'I fear you know nothing about it. If you

answer rightly, I shall look upon my official post as a thing of no consequence, much less will a little delay matter.'

" 'In that case, I may venture to trouble you with ·my inordinate chatter. The harpsichord was made by Fu Shi (the first of the fabulous Emperors of China, 2852–2737 B. C.). He saw that the virtue of the five planets was concentrated in the tung tree, and that the phoenix chose it for a resting-place. The phoenix is the king of birds, only eating bamboo sprouts, only drinking spring water. Fu Shi, therefore, seeing the princely nature of the tung tree, gathering into itself as it does the choicest essences of creation, argued that its wood might be expected to emit the choicest music. He therefore ordered a man to cut one down. This particular tree was 33 ft. 3 in. high, according with the number of the thirty-three heavens. He then had its trunk cut into three pieces, corresponding to the three powers of nature,—heaven, earth, man.

" 'On sounding the upper block it was found to ring with too high a note, while the lower block emitted too dull a sound. That of the middle block, however, was found to be a happy medium between the two. It was placed in a running stream for seventy-two days, according to the seventy-two periods of the year,—an ancient mode of division, each period being five days; then being dried in the shade, an exceptionally propitious time being chosen, and the Emperor employed a skilful workman to make it into a musical instrument.' "

At this stage Tung Chou Kion related how that a celebrated politician and man of letters named Ts'ai Yung (133–192), when a refugee in the State of Wu, was one day seated at the fireside when his attention was attracted by the sound emitted by a log of tung wood which lay burning there. Believing that its tones gave promise of rare excellence, he converted it into a lute. As the handle of his instrument still retained signs of scorching, it gave rise to the expression, "the scorching tail (lute)."

"In recent poetry," continued Chou Kion, "this incident is combined with that of Kung Peng Tah. A Hanyang poet sings—

'Now would I follow poesy and song,
Renewed in readiness the silken string,
My "heart's interpreter" at length has come.
The "scorched tail" interprets every wish;
The swiftly-flowing stream is heard once more,
Swells to the clouds the highest melody;

As whirlwinds now o'er myriad mountains borne,
Rises the melody sublime.'

"But to return to the story of the 'heart's interpreter referred to. The woodcutter proceeded: 'When completed, the harpsichord was thirty-six inches and a tenth long, according to the three hundred and sixty-one days in a (lunar) year. At the broad end it was eight inches across, according to the eight festivals; at the narrow end, four inches across, according to the four seasons. It was two inches thick, according to the masculine and feminine principles of nature. It had a golden youth's head and a gemmous maiden's waist, a back like that of an immortal, a dragon tank, and a phoenix bath. It had jade pegs and golden stops, which stops (let into the wood as a guide to the fingering) are thirteen, according to the twelve months of the year, plus the intercalary month.

" 'At first the harpsichord had five strings, according to the five elements, their sounds being called respectively Kung, Shang, Kioh, Tsz, and Yu (antediluvian tonic sol-fa!). In the time of the Emperors Yao and Shuin this five-stringed instrument was used to accompany the populace renovating odes of the day. A thousand years later, the literary monarch being in exile from his State, and lamenting over the death of his son Peh Yih-kao, added another string of pure and pathetic note, since called the literary string. Another son of his (almost a contemporary of King David) having defeated and slain the tyrant, and gained for himself the title of Military Monarch, added a seventh string, which is called after him.

" 'The harpsichord has six abhorrences and seven prohibitions. It abhors intense cold, intense heat, a high wind, a heavy rain, loud thunder, and a heavy fall of snow. It must not be played when wailing sounds are heard, when festive instruments are sounding, when the musician is worried, when his person is not clean, when his clothing is awry, without incense having first been lighted, or in the presence of an unsympathetic listener. Its eight excellencies in sound are purity, mystery, obscurity, choiceness, plaintiveness, energy, distance, and resonance. When played by a masterhand in the highest style, the howling tiger will listen, and cease its roar; the screaming monkey will listen, and cease its screeching.'

"Hearing the woodcutter discourse with such fluency and exactness, Kung Peng Tah imagined he must have learned it all by rote, but even then thought him a man not to be despised. Henceforth adopting politer form of speech, he essayed to test him a little farther. 'Confucius was once playing the harpsichord in the house,' he said, 'when Yen Hwui entered. As he listened to its deep and muffled tones, he thought he detected strains of blood-thirstiness, and asked in surprise whether it was so. Confucius answered, "As I was playing, I saw a cat chase a mouse, and smiled at the capture, but fearing it might lose its prey, my bloodthirstiness (!) betrayed itself on the silken strings." 'It was thus that the sacred and sensitive nature of music came to be fully known. Now, suppose I play my instrument with certain thoughts in my mind, can you recognize those thoughts as you listen?'

"Replied the woodcutter: 'In the Book of Odes it is written—

> "Another's thoughts
> I can fathom."

If you, sir, will extemporise a little, I will try and fathom your meaning. Should I guess wrong, pray pardon me.'

"Kung Peng Tah renewed the broken string and played a while, with mountain scenery in his mind. 'Excellent indeed!' exclaimed the other; 'your far-reaching thoughts were upon the high hills!' At which the musician could hardly believe his ears, and extemporized once more, with the rippling of hillside brooks in his mind. 'Excellent indeed!' cried the woodcutter; 'the flowing brooks are gurgling.'

"With the surprise that such thought interpretation might well call up, Peng Tah's brusqueness gave place to the geniality of a host, and the woodcutter had to take the place of honour on the left. With fervent apologies, Peng Tah exclaimed, 'Amid the rocks the princeless gem is hidden. 'And he who judges after the outward appearance and garb cannot fail to slight the most wisely virtuous everywhere.' Then, in the politest terms, he inquired the name of his guest. The reply, given in all humility was that his surname was Chung Tsz-ki, whereupon Peng Tah introduced himself.

"Tea was brought, then 'wine', and Peng Tah inquired after Tsz-ki's place of abode.

" 'Not far from here,' was the reply. 'I live beside the Horse Saddle Hill, in a hamlet called the Gathering-place of the Virtuous.' 'Truly so called!' exclaimed his host with inclined head. 'And what may your occupation be?'

" 'I cut wood for a living.'

" 'But how is it that with such abilities you do not seek for a degree, and an honourable official position instead of hiding your genius among hillside copses and streams, in the company of herdsmen and woodcutters? Why vegetate and wither when you might flourish as a scholar?'

" 'Because my parents are both stricken in years, and have no one else to provide for them. Had I the highest possible position offered me, I could not accept it, for they could not do without me for a single day.'

" 'Such a true son is hard to find,' exclaimed Peng Tah, whose affection for the young man was deepening. He asked how many 'spring-tides' he had passed? Tsz-ki replied that he had 'emptily passed' twenty-seven years. 'Then I am your senior by some ten odd years'—which was probably a polite understatement of fact. 'And if you will consent to such a relationship, I should like to call you brother, my never-to-be-forgotten thought-interpreter.'

"The meanly-clad young man looked at his friend in silk and fox furs, exclaiming, 'Surely you cannot mean it! You are a noted statesman of an honourable kingdom, and my lot is cast among the rustics. How could I venture to aspire to a friendship so incongruous and unbecoming?'

"To which Peng Tah replied that 'One's acquaintances may fill the earth, but heart interpreting friends are rare indeed. If I in my various vicissitudes,' he added tenderly, 'may be linked with you in the bonds of sworn brotherhood, it will be an unspeakable enrichment to my whole life.' Then almost pleadingly, 'If you think that I regard such things as riches and poverty as barriers, what manner of man do you take me to be?'

"Incense was added to the brazier, and thus at midnight, in the royally-furnished boat-chamber, the high statesman and the woodcutter went through the eight obeisances which would make them brothers forever. They were now known to each other by name.

"They changed seats, the elder brother taking the place of honour, and carried on their heart-to-heart conversation until the moon had declined and the stars began to pale. The boatmen having made all preparations for starting (some of them had doubtless been peeping through the window blinds in wonder), Tsz-ki rose to take his leave.

" 'My good brother,' said Kung Peng Tah,

'you and I have met too late, and, alas, must part thus early! At which Tsz-ki could not refrain his tears; and neither of them could bring his mind to the point of separation. 'My feelings are far from spent,' said the elder brother; 'could you not accompany me for a few days?'

" 'It is not for want of the will that I must decline,' replied the other; 'but how can I leave my aged parents? When the parents are alive, their children should not wander afar.' 'As they are both at home,' Peng Tah responded (with the rest of the quotation from the Analects as a basis for his words), 'could you not tell them you would like to go to Tsin to see your brother by and by? Thus, though "wandering afar," you would acquaint them with your whereabouts.'

" 'Not to grieve you,' Tsz-ki answered, 'I will not promise, and then break my word. But if I mention it to my parents, they will assuredly object to my going so far.'

" 'Let it be as you say, my noble brother. Then I will certainly come again next year and see you.'

" 'If you fix a date, I will be here ready to receive you.'

" 'Last night it was the mid-autumn festival. I shall be looking out for my brother on the fifteenth or sixteenth day of the mid-autumn month next year. I will not break my faith.' 'Then,' said Tsz-ki, 'I will be here on the river bank without fail. It is now daylight, and I must say farewell.'

" 'You must really go, my brother?' said Peng Tah, and he ordered the lad to bring two ingots of gold. These he presented to his brother with both hands, saying, 'This little gift will help towards the necessities of your parents. As you are bone of my bone and flesh of my flesh, you will not scorn to receive it.'

"Tsz-ki could not refuse, and took his departure; putting on his rain hat and grass cape, shouldering his spiked pole and sticking his hatchet in his girdle, he was handed along the plank to the shore. The boatmen beat the drums and started. The scenery was grand, but Peng Tah had no heart for it now. All his thoughts were with his heart's interpreter.

"Some days passed thus, and when he went ashore, and being recognized as a high official of Tsin, the mandarins of the port provided horses and carriages, accompanying him to the capital.

"Time flies apace! Autumn merged into winter; the spring and summer passed, but not for a single day had Peng Tah ceased to think of his brother. As the autumn was approaching, he petitioned the King of Tsin to allow him to go home a while. It was granted; and the fifteenth of the eighth moon found him once more near the Horse Saddle Hill. The boat was secured by grappling irons and a wooden stake driven into the bank.

"It was a lovely night; the moonbeams came stealing through the blinds. Peng Tah went out and stood on the deck. There was hardly a ripple on the waters. The northern constellation was clearly reflected on the glassy surface. Peng Tah opened his heart to the sweet serenity around, and the memories which the spot awakened. 'But my brother promised to be here on the bank waiting for me. There is no trace of him. Can he have broken his word? Nay, it cannot be. There are several boats about, and mine is not the same as I had last year. It was while playing my harpsichord that I discovered him. I will do so again, and he will hear the music and come.'

"So the sweet instrument was brought on deck, and that same brazier emitted clouds of perfume. The musician took the harpsichord out of its bag and tuned it, when one of the strings emitted a dirge-like note.

" 'How is this?' exclaimed Peng Tah. 'My brother must have some calamity in the house, and so he does not come. He told me both his parents were aged. One or other must be dead. He is a filial son, and has put the first claims first. He would rather break faith with me than neglect his parents, so he has not come. I will go on shore tomorrow and find him.'

"The instrument was brought in again, and he retired for the night. But not a moment's sleep could he get. He longed and looked for the morn. At length the moon declined, and the dawn was about to break over the hills. He arose, washed, and dressed himself, putting on plain garments, and, with the lad bearing his harpsichord and a large quantity of gold, he went ashore. 'If my brother have any mourning in the house,' he said, 'this will cover the ceremonies required of the filial.'

"He walked on until he came to the end of the valley, where he stood still. The road divided to the east and the west, but no trace of the hamlet he sought. He sat upon a wayside rock for a while, when an old man with a long, white, silky beard came along, leaning upon his staff. Peng Tah advanced to meet him, and asked which of the two roads led to the desired village.

" 'There are two villages of that name, an upper and a lower,' the old man replied; 'which one was it you wished to visit?' "

" 'My brother is a clear-headed man,' thought Peng Tah; 'why did he speak thus ambiguously? I have it! He did not mean to put me to the trouble of seeking him out.' "

" 'Your silence, sir, indicates that the person who directed you did not seem to know of the existence of two villages, which are in opposite directions from here. I have lived on the hillside for many a long year, and know everyone here as neighbours or relatives or else as friends. What is the name of the person you are seeking?'

" 'I wish to find out the house of the Chung family.'

" 'To seek for whom?'

" 'To find out Tsz-ki.'

"At this the old man's eyes filled with tears. He sobbed out. 'My own son! Last year at this time, as he was out cutting wood, he met a statesman of Tsin, named Kung Peng Tah, who became attached to him, presenting him with two ingots of gold as he went away. My son bought many books and studied hard, so as to be worthy of his kindness.   Returning with his heavy faggots, he would read on into the night, until he fell ill and—after—some—months—he—died!'

With a loud cry Peng Tah fell down in a swoon.   The old man did his best, with the lad's assistance, to restore him; and asked who the traveller was.   The lad whispered in his ear, 'The statesman, Kung Peng Tah himself.'

"As consciousness returned, Peng Tah wailed bitterly, 'My brother! my brother!   There was I on the boat last night talking of broken promises! Little did I think that you were gone!'   He rose and saluted the old man, asking whether his son was already buried or not.

" 'It cannot be told in one word,' the old man replied.   'As my son was dying, and we were watching at his bedside, he said, "The bounds of my life have been fixed by Heaven.   I cannot fulfill my earthly relations.   But I beseech you, bury me by and by on the bank near the place where I met the good statesman, so that I may keep my promise with him."   Along the road you came there is a new grave by the wayside. It is my son's.   I was just going to visit it.'

" 'I will accompany you.'

"They preceeded along the path, the aged father and the elder brother, until they reached the grave, when Peng Tah's sobs broke out afresh. 'My brother,' he cried, 'thou art among the higher intelligences now. I bid thee a long farewell.' Thus he wailed until the country folk assembled. They found out who he was, and crowded to the front to stare at the man in his anguish.

"The sweet-toned instrument was taken out of its bag, and with streaming eyes Peng Tah played a dirge. The sightseers, hearing the music by the grave side, went off clapping their hands in merriment. The musician asked the reason, when he was through bewailing his brother. To which the old man replied that the rustics, not discerning his meaning, took the notes to be festal strains.

" 'Can that be so? At least you will interpret my heart's meaning?'

" 'Alas! I am stupid and dull. I played the harpsichord when I was younger, but now in my old age my five senses are half gone.'

" 'I have been extemporizing a heart-prompted dirge. I will sing it once for you to hear.'

"With tremulous voice the statesman sang—

'I recall the fond hopes of last year,
When my friend on the bank I met here;
I have come back to see him again,
I have come back to see him in vain.
But a heap of cold earth do I find,
And sore is my sorrow-filled mind;
My sore heart is stricken with grief,
My tears are my only relief.
I came here in joy; with what grief do I go!
The banks of the river are clouded with woe.
Tsz-ki! my lost Tsz-ki!
True as tried gold were we.
Beyond the heavenly shore
Thy voice I hear no more.
I sing thee my last song, my last.
The harpsichord's music is past.'

"Then, taking a small knife from his girdle, he cut the silken strings in twain, and lifting the instrument with both hands, as if in sacrifice, he put forth all his strength, and dashed it to pieces upon the grave.

"The old man wonderingly asked the reason for this.

" 'Tsz-ki is gone; to whom should I play now? Springtime friends abound, but to find a heart's interpreter is a difficulty of difficulties.'

" 'I am too sad,' Peng Tah continued, 'to accompany you home, but have brought with me some gold, half of which will minister to your present needs, and half will buy a little land around, so that (from the crops thereon) the grave may be ever kept in repair. If you will wait till I return to my adopted country, and ask leave to retire from office, I will come and fetch my venerable father and mother to the old home, there to be cared for until the appointed years of Heaven are fulfilled. I was one with Tsz-ki and he with me. Do not think of me as an outsider'; and he handed the gold to the old man, who re‧ceived it with tearful gratitude.

"A few months after, each had gone his way."

Among Tung Chou Kion's rustic audience were sympathetic listeners, and more than one sleeve was applied to moist eyes. The narrator himself was not unmoved. He added, with emotion, "I visited the grave to weep there a while."

Subdued to silence, the company dispersed.

"My princely husband," said his wife after a pause, "I am 'but a woman,' yet may I be reckoned as your heart's interpreter? I will sympathise in your wrongs, and share your coming joys."

THE PAINTED CAT
Told by
LING WANG

"Have you heard of the painted cat which caught mice? Well, I will tell you the tale." He accordingly related the following between the mouthfuls of the supper which Kno Tzu Chien began to provide as an institution. "There was once a fortune-teller who used to sit near the gate of a large yamun. He had the reputation of being a man of great ability and accuracy, and the high mandarin at whose door he sat believed in him thoroughly.

"A young water coolie of the place once asked him to tell his fortune well, and offered him eight hundred cash for the job. He had forgotten his eight characters' (year, month, day, and hour of birth), but having received such a sum, the fortune-teller agreed to find eight propitious characters for him. From these he prophesied that there was a princedom in store for him. The coolie took the paper, but soon afterwards dropped it.

"The mandarin being very particular about reverencing written paper, had his bearers pick up a piece lying on the street before them, read it, and found that there was a high destiny a-waiting the young coolie. He had him called in, set him to study, and eventually gave him his daughter in marriage.

"The fortunate young man, however, was in the habit of exclaiming, 'Worth eight hundred cash! Well worth eight hundred cash!' the meaning of which he could not divulge to his wife. One day, however, the exclamation hav-ing been made in the mandarin's presence, he had to confess that it referred to the somewhat manipulated document the fortune-teller gave him. At this the enraged mandarin tried to make his daughter give up her husband. She re-fused, and he put them into a rudderless boat on the sea. The boat drifted on until it stranded at length on a rocky island which was strewn with remarkable stones.

"These they gathered till the boat could hold no more, then set sail again, reaching a certain land where was a large city. The faithful wife left her husband in charge of the boat, went on shore, and soon found a large curio shop, the wares of which attracted her attention, especially a painting of a cat which hung from the wall. This so struck her fancy, that she returned to exhort her husband to try and procure it. A crowd followed her, and collected around the boat, jabbering in some unknown tongue.

"After inspecting the cargo, the inhabitants of this foreign realm seemed evidently to be asking the price. Instructed by his wife, the man held up five fingers, which at length was rightly interpreted to mean five hundred ounces of silver. Further signs were made to show that the picture of the cat must be given in. It was done, and they set sail again.

"Fortune brought them eventually to a city upon the shores of China, from whence the former water-carrier proceeded home with his wife, but they were treated very shabbily, being put into a stable. Here, however, they learnt that they had no ordinary 'treasure' in their picture; and after a while, proclamations were posted everywhere to say that the Emperor was troubled by the ravages of an enormous rat, which had killed many a cat. He offered high rewards to the man who would rid the palace of the insufferable pest. Hearing of which, the wife advised the husband to go off to the capital with his picture. He did so, gaining an Imperial interview. Having fixed the scroll upon the wall, he watched beside it at night. The rat proceeded as of old,

but the cat leaped from the scroll and killed it.
Whereupon the Emperor made the man a prince
of the realm. A good tale, is it not?"

"Is it all true, do you think?"

"True? Who said it was? Nothing is true
nowadays. I don't believe in anything—except
myself, and your suppers."

THE FISHERMAN

Told by

YOUNG LEE

In the northern part of Tzŭ-chou there lived
a man named Hsü, a fisherman by trade. Every
night when he went to fish, he would carry some
wine with him, and drink and fish by turns, always taking care to pour out a libation on the
ground, accompanied by the following invocation
—"Drink too, ye drowned spirits of the river!"
Such was his regular custom; and it was also
noticeable that, even on occasions when the other
fishermen caught nothing, he always got a full
basket. One night, as he was sitting drinking by
himself, a young man suddenly appeared and began walking up and down near him. Hsü
offered him a cup of wine, which was readily accepted, and they remained chatting together
throughout the night, Hsü meanwhile not catch-

HSU THE FISHERMAN

ing a single fish. However, just as he was giving up all hope of doing anything, the young man rose and said he would go a little way down the stream and beat them up towards Hsü, which he accordingly did returning in a few minutes and warning him to be on the lookout. Hsü now heard a noise like that of a shoal coming up the stream, and casting his net, made a splendid haul, —all that he caught being over a foot in length. Greatly delighted, he now prepared to go home, first offering his companion a share of the fish, which the latter declined, saying that he had often received kindnesses from Mr. Hsü, and that he would be only too happy to help him regularly in the same manner if Mr. Hsü would accept his assistance. The latter replied that he did not recollect ever meeting him before, and that he should be much obliged for any aid the young man might choose to afford him, regretting, at the same time, his inability to make him any adequate return. He then asked the young man his name and surname; and the young man said his surname was Wang, adding that Hsü might address him when they met as Wang Liulang, he having no other name. Thereupon they parted, and the next day Hsü sold his fish and bought some more wine, with which he repaired as usual to the river-bank. There he found his companion already awaiting him, and they spent the night together in precisely the same way as the preceding one, the young man beating up the fish for him as before. This went on for some months, until at length one evening the young man, with many expressions of his thanks and his regrets, told Hsü that they were about to part for ever. Much alarmed by the melancholy tone in which his friend had communicated this news, Hsü was on the point of asking for an explanation, when the young man stopped him, and himself proceeded as follows:—"The friendship that has grown up between us is truly surprising, and, now that we shall meet no more, there is no harm in telling you the whole truth. I am a disembodied spirit—the soul of one who was drowned in this river when tipsy. I have been here many years, and your former success in fishing was due to the fact that I used secretly to beat up the fish towards you, in return for the libations you were accustomed to pour out. To-morrow my time is up: my substitute will arrive, and I shall be born again in the world of mortals. We have but this one evening left, and I therefore take advantage of it to express my feelings to you." On hearing these words, Hsü was at first very much alarmed; however, he had grown so accustomed to his friend's society, that his fears soon passed away; and, filling up a goblet, he said, with a sigh, "Liu-lang, old fellow, drink this up, and away with melancholy. It's hard to lose you; but I'm glad enough for your sake, and won't think of my own sorrow." He then inquired of Liu-lang who was to be his substitute; to which the latter replied, "Come to the river-bank to-morrow afternoon and you'll see a woman drowned; she is the one." Just then the village cocks began to crow, and, with tears in their eyes, the two friends bade each other farewell.

Next day Hsü waited on the river-bank to see if anything would happen, and lo! a woman carrying a child in her arms came along. When close to the edge of the river, she stumbled and fell into the water, managing, however, to throw the child safely on to the bank, where it lay kicking and sprawling and crying at the top of its voice. The woman herself sank and rose several times, until at last she succeeded in clutching hold of the bank and pulled herself out; and then, after resting awhile, she picked up the child and went on her way. All this time Hsü had been in a great state of excitement, and was on the point of running to help the woman out of the water; but he remembered that she was the substitute of his friend, and accordingly re-restrained himself from doing so. Then when he saw the woman get out by herself, he began to suspect that Liu-lang's words had not been ful-filled. That night he went to fish as usual, and before long the young man arrived and said, "We meet once again: there is no need now to speak of separation." Hsü asked him how it was so; to which he replied, "The woman you saw had al-ready taken my place, but I could not bear to hear the child cry, and I saw that my own life would be purchased at the expense of their two lives, wherefore I let her go, and now I cannot say when I shall have another chance. The un-ion of our destinies may not yet be worked out." "Alas!" sighed Hsü, "this noble conduct of yours is enough to move God Almighty."

After this the two friends went on much as they had done before, until one day Liu-lang again said he had come to bid Hsü farewell. Hsü thought he had found another substitute, but Liu-lang told him that his former behaviour had so pleased Almighty Heaven, that he had been appointed guardian angel of Wu-chên, in the Chao-yüan district, and that on the following

morning he would start for his new post. "And
if you do not forget the days of our friendship,"
added he, "I pray you come and see me, in spite
of the long journey." "Truly," replied Hsü,
"you well deserved to be made a God; but the
paths of Gods and men lie in different directions,
and even if the distance were nothing, how should
I manage to meet you again?" "Don't be afraid
on that score," said Liu-lang, "but come"; and
then he went away, and Hsü returned home. The
latter immediately began to prepare for the journey, which caused his wife to laugh at him and
say, "Supposing you do find such a place at the
end of that long journey, you won't be able to
hold a conversation with a clay image." Hsü,
however, paid no attention to her remarks, and
travelled straight to Chao-Yüan, where he had
learned from the inhabitants that there really
was a village called Wuchên, whither he forthwith proceeded and took up his abode at an inn.
He then inquired of the landlord where the village temple was; to which the latter replied by
asking him somewhat hurriedly if he was speaking to Mr. Hsü. Hsü informed him that his
name was Hsü, asking in reply how he came to
know it; whereupon the landlord further inquired if his native place was not Tzŭ-chou.

Hsü told him it was, and again asked him how he knew all this; to which the landlord made no answer, but rushed out of the room; and in a few moments the place was crowded with old and young, men, women, and children, all come to visit Hsü. They then told him that a few nights before they had seen their guardian deity in a vision, and he had informed them that Mr. Hsü would shortly arrive, and had bidden them to provide him with travelling expenses. Hsü was very much astonished at this, and went off at once to the shrine, where he invoked his friend as follows:—"Ever since we parted I have had you daily and nightly in my thoughts; and now that I have fulfilled my promise of coming to see you, I have to thank you for the orders you have issued to the people of the place. As for me, I have nothing to offer you but a cup of wine, which I pray you accept as though we were drinking together on the river-bank." He then burnt a quantity of paper money, when lo! a wind suddenly arose, which after whirling round and round behind the shrine, soon dropped and all was still. That night Hsü dreamed that his friend came to him, dressed in his official cap and robes, and very different in appearance from what he used to be, and thanked him saying, "It is truly kind of you to visit me thus: I only regret that my position makes me unable to meet you face to face, and that though near we are still so far. The people here will give you a trifle, which pray accept for my sake; and when you go away, I will see you a short way on your journey." A few days afterwards Hsü prepared to start, in spite of the numerous invitations to stay which poured in upon him from all sides; and then the inhabitants loaded him with presents of all kinds, and escorted him out of the village. There a whirlwind arose and accompanied him several miles, when he turned round and invoked his friend thus:—"Liu-Lang, take care of your valued person. Do not trouble yourself to come any farther. Your noble heart will ensure happiness to this district, and there is no occasion for me to give a word of advice to my old friend." By-and-by the whirlwind ceased, and the villagers, who were much astonished, returned to their own homes. Hsü, too, travelled homewards, and being now a man of some means, ceased to work any more as a fisherman. And whenever he met a Chao-yüan man he would ask him about that guardian angel, being always informed in reply that he was a most beneficent God. Some say the place was Shih-k'êng-chuang, in Chang-ch'in: I can't say which it was myself.

PART II

TAOIST TALES

Told at

A TAO ANNIVERSARY

F RIENDS!" said Kno Tzu Chien, to the gathering at his lodge on the occasion of an evening devoted to Taoist lore: "we are here to-night to pay tribute to the memory of the great sage Lao-Tzu, founder of Taoism and author of the most Sacred Book, the Tao Teh King— which might mean Book of Nature's Way.

"Lao-Tzu, or the aged philosopher, was born 604 B. C. in the Province of Houan and popular tradition tells us he was eighty-one years at birth, had Snowy White hair and the appearance of an aged Saint. He called people back to nature saying: 'Never yet become so unnatural that the natural looks unnatural, and the unnatural looks natural to you: Rather say to yourself 'If Nature is good enough for the spirit of Heaven it should be good enough for the human.' Again he says: 'Man takes his laws from the earth; the earth takes its laws from Heaven; Heaven takes its laws from the Tao, and the Tao takes its laws from what is in itself—the spirit of the Tao or the first cause.' We have in the gathering, here this evening, many very old and most honorable sages who will tell us some of the Taoist tales that they heard from their elders, when they were in their youth.

"Lao Tzu himself said: 'The Tao that can be defined is not the true Tao.' Yet he tells us: 'When man follows the dictates of his higher nature his actions are good, and harmony results. When he is unduly influenced by the outward world his actions are evil, and discords come into his life. The true Taoist is one who has an instinctive inward sight of the ultimate principle in its twofold operation, or what might be called the sight of the Heaven Spirit—the beatific vision, and who has the cosmic spirit within, which makes it easy to sense and obey nature.' One who has this cosmic pulse is perfectly wise; his action perfectly good; and his words perfectly true;—for he is in the Tao, and the Tao is the flow of the divine Spirit in human life.

"I will now ask the Honorable Taoist Sage, Kang Yang Ti, if he will honor us in opening the evening's Story-telling by giving us a Taoist description of the place where dwells the Spirit of our honorable ancestors.

THE TAOIST'S DESCRIPTION OF HEAVEN

Told by

KANG LANG TI

The Taoist, having ascended to the boundary on high, he all at once saw the halls of heaven, where golden light spirited forth its ruddy rainbows in a myriad directions, while the felicitous air breathed out a thousand streams of purple vapour.

The southern gate of heaven was of the deepest emerald glass, glistening and lucent, as if fused in a precious cauldron. On either side were four massive pillars, around which twined pink-bearded dragons, cloud-riding and mist-dispersing. In the midst were two jade bridges, standing whereon were the cloud-aspiring phoenixes, with irridescent plumage and cinnabar-coloured crests, mid glistening beams of ruby sunset light, and emerald vapours, which obscured the starry constellations and the light of day.

There are thirty-three pavilions in heaven; the cloud-dividing pavilion, the wave-collecting pavilion, the purple sunset pavilion, the pavilion of the sun, the pavilion of the moon, the pavilion of ever-renewing pleasure among them. Each pavilion is ceiled with the teeth of the celestial stag.

There are seventy-two tiers of palaces, by the pillars of which stand ranks of jade unicorns. There is the star of longevity tower, the star of emolument tower, and the star of happiness tower. At their bases are wondrous flowers, ,which fade not in a thousand thousand years. There is the immortality pill brazier, the eight diagrams brazier and the water-fire brazier. Between these springs which are verdant and flourishing for a myriad myriad years.

Within the sacred palaces the robes of the blessed are of rose-coloured gauze. Beneath the vermilion throne steps are they whose headgear is like the mallow flower. That temple of living empyrean! The golden dragons crowd through its jade portals. Those sacred towers! The phoenixes leap by the jade-hewn gates, moving in and out along corridors ornate with translucent tracery. Triple colonnades! Quadruple mansions! Ranks upon ranks of dragons and phoenixes soaring hither and thither. And high above all flash beams of purple light. Clear their splendour; brilliant with many a scintillation. A clear clanging sound proceeds from the neck of the magic gourd. On every hand are heard tinklings varied and confused, laminated sounds as of gurgling and dripping, brightly sonorous like those of the jade pendants of the courtiers.

Truly wondrous the sights and sounds of heaven, so rarely known on earth. Golden portals of paradise; silvery courts majestic; purple halls; wondrous flowers, strange herbs fill the jasper realm, far beneath whose audience chambers courses the gemmous hare (the moon, you know) ; far beneath where they bow before the sacred majesty flies the golden crow (the sun, of course). He who has the felicity to reach the heavenly boundary will never grovel again in the filthy mud of earth.

Here a dog barked, and the hens cackled, which drew forth the remark that a Taoist philosopher (Hwai Nan-tsz—died B. C. 122) attained to such merit, that when he ascended the skies his chickens and dogs ascended with him.

The household then retired to rest, and probably to dream of invisible men and of heaven.

A TAOIST EXPLAINS LOVE
Told by
MAH TI

It was evening, and I sat with a Taoist sage upon the soft turf of the mountain-side, the quietness of our mood in sympathy with the solemn stillness of twilight. The distant mountain-ranges reposed in an atmosphere breathing reverence and devotion—they seemed to be kneeling beneath the heavens, beneath the slow-descending blessing of night. The isolated trees dotted here and there about the hills stood motionless, in a pause of silent worshipping. The rush of the sea sounded distant and indistinct, lost in its own greatness. Peace lay over everything, and soft sounds went up, as of prayer.

The hermit sat beside me, dignified as a tree in the midst of Nature, and awe-inspiring as the evening itself.

I had returned to question him again. For my soul found no repose apart from him, and a mighty impulse was stirring within me. But now that I found myself near him, I hardly dared to speak; and indeed it seemed as though words were no longer necessary—as though everything lay, of itself, open and clear as daylight. How goodly and simple everything appeared that evening! Was it not my own inmost being that I recognized in all the beauty around me? And was not the whole on the point of being absorbed into the Eternal?

Nevertheless I broke in upon this train of feeling, and cleft the peaceful silence with my voice:

"Father," I said sadly, "all your words have sunk into my mind, and my soul is filled with the balm of them. This soul of mine is no longer my own—no longer what I used to be. It is as though I were dead: And I know not what is taking place within me—by day and by night— causing it to grow so light, and clear, and vacant in my mind. Father, I know it is Tao; it is death, and glorious resurrection; but it is not love; and without love, Tao appears to me but a gloomy lie."

The old man looked round him at the evening scene, and smiled gently.

"What is love?" he asked calmly. "Are you sure about that, I wonder?"

"No, I am not sure," I answered. "I do not know anything about it, but that is just the reason for its great blessedness. Yes, do but let me express it! I mean: love of a maiden, love of a woman.—I remember yet, Father, what it was to me when I saw the maiden, and my soul knew delight for the first time. It was like a sea, like a broad heaven, like death. It was light —and I had been blind! It had hurt, Father— my heart beat so violently—and my eyes burned. The world was afire, and all things were strange, and began to live. It was a great flame flaring from out my soul. It was so fearful, but so lovely, and so infinitely great! Father, I think it was greater than Tao!"

"I know well what it was," said the sage. "It was Beauty, the earthly form of the formless Tao, calling up in you the rythm of that move- ment by which you will enter into Tao. You might have experienced the same at sight of a tree, a cloud, a flower. But because you are hu- man, living by desire, therefore to you it could only be revealed through another human being, a woman—because, also, that form is to you more easily understood, and more familiar. And since desire did not allow the full upgrowth of a pure contemplation, therefore was the rhythm within you wrought up to be wild tempest, like a storm- thrashed sea that knows not whither it is tending. The inmost essence of the whole emotion was not 'love,' but Tao."

But the calmness of the old sage made me impatient, and excited me to answer roughly:

"It is easy to talk thus theoretically, but seeing that you have never experienced it yourself,
you can understand nothing of that of which you
speak!"

He looked at me steadily, and laid his hand
sympathetically on my shoulder.

"It would be cruel of you to speak thus to any
one but me, young man!— I loved, before you
drew breath in this world. At that time there
lived a maiden, so wondrous to see, it was as if
she were the direct-born expression of Tao. For
me she was the world, and the world lay dead
around her. I saw nothing but her, and for me
there existed no such things as trees, men, or
clouds. She was more beautiful than this evening, gentler than the lines of those distant mountains, more tender than those hushed tree-tops;
and the light of her presence was more pleasant
to see than the still shining of yonder star. I
will not tell you her story. It was more scorching than a very hell-fire—but it was not real, and
it is over now, like a storm that has passed. It
seemed to me that I must die; I longed to flee
from my pain into death.— But there came a
dawning in my soul, and all grew light and com-
prehensible. Nothing was lost. All was yet as

it had been. The beauty which I believed had been taken from me lived on still, spotless, in myself. For not from this woman,—out of my soul had this beauty sprung; and this I saw shining yet, all over the world, with an everlasting radiance, Nature was no other than what I had fashioned to myself out of that shadowy form of a woman. And my soul was one with Nature, and floated with a like rhythm towards the eternal Tao."

Calmed by his calmness, I said: "She whom I loved is dead, Father— She who culled my soul as a child culls a flower never became my wife. But I have a wife now, a miracle of strength and goodness, a wife who is essential to me as light and air. I do not love her as I even now love the dead. But I know that she is a purer human being than that other. How is it then that I do not love her so much? She has transformed my wild and troubled life into a tranquil march towards death. **Love is the Tao.** She is simple and true as Nature itself, and her face is dear to me as the sunlight."

"You love her, indeed!" said the sage, "but you know not what love means, nor loving. I will tell it you. Love is no other than the rhythm of Tao. I have told you: you are come out of Tao, and to Tao you will return. Whilst you are young—with your soul still enveloped in darkness—the shock of the first impulse within you, you know not yet whither you are trending. You see the woman before you. You believe her to be that towards which the rhythm is driving you. But even when the woman is yours, and you have thrilled at the touch of her, you feel the rhythm yet within you, unappeased, and know that you must forward, ever further, if you would bring it to a standstill. Then it is that in the soul of the man and of the woman there arises a great sadness, and they look at one another, questioning whither they are now bound. Gently they clasp one another by the hand, and move on through life, swayed by the same impulse, towards the same goal. Call this love if you will. What is a name? I call it Tao. And the souls of those who love are like two white clouds floating softly side by side, that vanish, wafted by the same wind, into the infinite blue of the heavens."

"But that is not the love that I mean!" I cried. "Love is not the desire to see the loved one absorbed into Tao; love is the longing to be always with her; the deep yearning for the blending of two souls in one; the hot desire to soar, in one breath with her, into felicity. And this always with the loved ones alone—not with others, not with Nature. And, were I absorbed into Tao, all this happiness would be for ever lost! Oh, let me stay here, in this goodly world, with my faithful companion! Here it is so bright and homely, and Tao is still so gloomy and inscrutable for me."

"The hot desire dies out," he answered calmly. "The body of our loved one will wither and pass away within the cold earth. The leaves of the trees fade in autumn, and the withered flowers droop sadly to the ground. How can you love that so much which does not last? However, you know in truth, as yet, neither how you love nor what it is that you love. The beauty of woman is but a vague reflection of the formless beauty of Tao. The emotion it awakens, the longing to lose yourself in her beauty, that ecstasy of feeling which would lend wings for the flight of your soul with the beloved—beyond horizon-bounds, into regions of bliss—believe me, it is no other than the rhythm of Tao; only you know it not. You resemble still the river which knows as yet only its shimmering banks; which has no knowledge of the power that draws it forward; but which will one day inevitably flow out into the great ocean.

Why this striving after happiness, after human happiness, that lasts but a moment and then vanishes again? Chuang-Tse said truly: 'The highest happiness is no happiness.' Is it not small and pitiable, this momentary uprising, and downfalling, and uprising again? This wavering, weakly intention and progress of men? Do not seek happiness in a woman. She is the joyful revelation of Tao directed towards you. She is the purest form in the whole of nature by which Tao is manifested. She is the gentle force that awakens the rhythm of Tao within you. But she is only a poor creature like yourself. And you are for her the same joyful revelation that she is to you. Fancy not that that which you perceive in her is that Tao, that very holiest into which you would one day ascend! For then you would surely reject her when you realized what she was. If you will truly love a woman, then love her as a being of the same poor nature as yourself, and do not seek happiness with her. Whether in your love you see this or not—her inmost being is Tao. A poet looks upon a woman, and, swayed by 'rhythm,' he perceives the beauty of the beloved in all things—in the trees, the mountains, the horizon; for the beauty of a woman is the same as that of Nature. It is the form of Tao, the great and formless, and what your soul desires in the excitement of beholding—this strange, unspeakable feeling—is nothing but your oneness with this beauty, and with the source of this beauty—Tao. And the like is experienced by your wife. Ye are for each other angels, who lead one another to Tao unconsciously."

I was silent for a while, reflecting. In the soft colouring and stillness of the evening lay a great sadness. About the horizon, where the sun had set, there glimmered a streak of faint red light, like dying pain.

"What is this sadness, then, in the Nature around us?" I asked. "Is there not that in the twilight as though the whole earth were weeping with a grievous longing? See how she mourns, with these fading hues, these drooping tree-tops, and solemn mountains. Human eyes must fill with tears, when this great grief of Nature looms within their sight. It is as though she were longing for her beloved—as though everything—seas, mountains and heavens—were full of mourning."

And the Sage replied: "It is the same pain which cries in the hearts of men. Your own longing quivers in Nature too. The Spirit of the evening is also the Spirit of your soul. Your soul has lost her love: Tao, with whom she once was one; and your soul desires re-union with her love. Absolute re-union with Tao—is not that an immense love?—to be so absolutely one with the beloved that you are wholly hers, she wholly yours;—a union so full and eternal that neither death nor life can ever cleave your oneness again? So tranquil and pure that desire can no more awaken in you—perfect blessedness being attained, and a holy and permanent peace? For Tao is one single, eternal, pure infinitude of soul.

"Is that not more perfect than the love of a woman?—this poor, sad love, each day of which reveals to you some sullying of the clear life of the soul by dark and sanguine passion. When you are absorbed into Tao, then only will you be completely, eternally united with the soul of your beloved, with the souls of all men, your brothers, and with the soul of Nature. And the few moments of blessedness fleetingly enjoyed by all lovers upon earth are as nothing in comparison with that endless bliss: the blending of the souls of all who love in an eternity of perfect purity."

A horizon of blessedness opened out before my

soul, wider than the vague horizon of the sea, wider than the heavens.

"Father!" I cried in ecstasy, "can it be that everything is so holy? I have never known it—I have been so filled with longing, and so worn out with weeping; and my breast has been heavy with sobs and dread. I have been so consumed with fear! I have trembled at the thought of death! I have despaired of all things being good, when I saw so much suffering around me. I have believed myself damned, by reasons of the wild passions, the bodily desires, burning within and flaming without me—passions which, though hating them, I still was, coward-like, condemned to serve. With what breathless horror I have realized how the tender, flower-like body of my love must one day moulder and crumble away in the cold, dark earth! I have believed that I should never feel again that blessed peace at the look in her eyes, through which her soul was shining. And was it Tao!—was Tao really even then always within me, like a faithful guardian? And was it Tao that shone from her eyes? Was Tao in everything that surrounded me? in the clouds, the trees and the sea? Is the inmost being of earth and heaven, then, also the inmost being of my beloved and my own soul? Is it that for which there burns within me that mysterious longing which I did not understand, and which drove me so restlessly onward? I thought it was leading me away from the beloved and that I was ceasing to love her!— Was it really the rhythm of Tao, then, that moved my beloved too?—the same as that in which all nature breathes, and all suns and planets pursue their shining course throughout eternity?— Then all is indeed made holy!—then Tao is indeed in everything, as my soul is in Tao! Oh, Father, Father! it is growing so light in my heart! My soul seems to foresee that which will come one day; and the heavens above us, and the great sea, they foretell it too! See, how reverent is the pose of these trees around us—and see the lines of the mountains, how soft in their holy repose! **The Tao is in all things.** All nature is filled with sacred awe, and my soul, too, thrills with ecstacy, for she has looked upon her beloved!"

I sat there long, in silent, still forgetfulness. It was to me as though I were one with the soul of my master and with nature. I saw nothing and heard nothing;—void of all desire, bereft of all will, I lay sunk in the deepest peace. I was awakened by a soft sound close by me. A fruit had fallen from the tree to the ground behind us.

When I looked up, it was into shimmering moonlight. The recluse was standing by me, and bent over me kindly.

"You have strained your spirit overmuch, my young friend!" he said concernedly. "It is too much for you in so short a time. You have fallen asleep from exhaustion. The sea sleeps too. See, not a furrow breaks its even surface; motionless, dreaming, it receives the benediction of the light. But you must awaken! It is late, your boat is ready, and your wife awaits you at home in the town."

I answered, still half dreaming: "I would so gladly stay here. Let me return, with my wife, and stay here for ever! I cannot go back to the people again! Ah, Father, I shudder—I can see their scoffing faces, their insulting glances, their disbelief, and their irreverence! How can I ever so hide it under smile or speech that they shall never detect it, nor desecrate it with their insolent ridicule?"

Then, laying his hand earnestly upon my shoulder, he said:

"Listen carefully to what I now say to you, my friend, and above all, believe me. I shall give you pain, but I cannot help it. You must return to the world and your fellow-men; it cannot be otherwise. You have spoken too much with me already; perhaps I have said somewhat too much to you. Your further growth must be your own doing, and you must find out everything for yourself. Be only simple of heart, and you will discover everything without effort, like a child finding flowers. At this moment you feel deeply and purely what I have said to you. This present mood is one of the highest moments of your life. But you cannot yet be strong enough to maintain it. You will relapse, and spiritual feeling will turn again to words and theories.

Only by slow degrees will you grow once more to feel it purely and keep it permanently. When that is so, then you may return hither in peace and then you will do well to remain here; —but by that time I shall be long dead.

"**You must complete your growth in the midst of life, not outside it;** for you are not yet pure enough to rise above it. A moment ago, it is true, you were equal even to that, but the reaction will soon set in. You may not shun the rest of mankind; they are your equals, even though they may not feel so purely as you do. You can go amongst them as their comrade, and take them by the hand; only do not let them look upon your soul, so long as they are still so far behind you. They would not mock you from evil-mindedness, but rather out of religious persuasion, being unaware how utterly miserable, how godless, how forsaken, they are, and how far from all those holy things by which you actually live. You must be so strong in your conviction that nothing can hinder you. And that you will only become after a long and bitter struggle. But out of your tears will grow your strength, and through your pain you will attain peace. Above all remember that Tao, Poetry and Love are one and the same, although you may seek to define it by these several vague terms;—and that it is always within you and around you;—that it never forsakes you; and that you are safe and well cared for in this holy environment. You are surrounded with benefits, and sheltered by a love which is eternal. Everything is rendered holy through the primal force of Tao dwelling within it."

He spoke so gently and convincingly that I had no answer to give. Willingly I allowed myself to be guided by him to the shore. My boat lay motionless upon the smooth water, awaiting me.—

"Farewell, my young friend! Farewell!" he

said, calmly and tenderly. "Remember all that I have told you!"

But I could not leave him in such a manner. Suddenly I thought of the loneliness of his life in this place, and tears of sympathy rose to my eyes. I grasped his hand.

"Father, come with me!" I besought him. "My wife and I will care for you, we will do everything for you; and when you are sick we will tend you. Do not stay here in this loneliness, so void of all the love that might make life sweet to you!"

He smiled gently, and shook his head as a father might at some fancy of his child's, answering with tranquil kindness:

"You have lapsed already! Do you realize now how necessary it is for you to remain in the midst of every-day life? I have but this moment told you how great is the love which surrounds me—and still you deem me lonely here and forsaken?—Here, in Tao, I am as safe at home as a child is with its mother. You mean it well, my friend, but you must grow wiser, much wiser! Be not concerned for me; that is unnecessary, grateful though I am to you for this feeling. Think of yourself just now. And do what I say. Believe that I tell you that which is best for you. In the boat lies something which should remind you of the days you have spent here. Farewell!"

I bent silently over his hand and kissed it. I thought I felt that it trembled with emotion; but when I looked at him again his face was calm and cheerful as the moon in the sky.

I stepped into the boat, and the boatman took up the oars. With dextrous strokes he drove it over the even surface of the water. I was already some way from the land when my foot struck against some object in the boat and I remember that something for me was lying there. I took it up. It was a small chest. Hastily I lifted the lid. And in the soft, calm moonlight there gleamed with mystical radiance the wonderful porcelain of the Kwan-Yin image, the same which the old man had cherished so carefully, and loved so well.

There, in the lofty tranquility of severe yet gentle lines, in all the ethereal delicacy of the transparent porcelain, reposed the pure figure of Kwan-Yin, shining as with spiritual radiance amidst the shimmering petals of the lotus.

I scarcely dared believe that this holy thing had been given to me. I seized my handkerchief, and waved with it towards the shore, to convey to the recluse my thanks. He stood there motionless, gazing straight before him. I waited longingly for him to wave—for one more greeting from him—one more sign of love—but he remained immovable.

Was it I after whom he was gazing? Was he gazing at the sea? . . .

I closed the lid of the chest, and kept it near me, as though it had been a love of his which I was bearing away. I knew that he cared for me; but his imperturbable serenity was too great for me—it saddened my mood that he had never signed to me again.

We drew further and further away; the outlines of his figure grew fainter and fainter; at last I could see it no more.

He remained; with the dreams of his soul, in the midst of nature—alone in infinity—bereft of all human love—but close to the great bosom of Tao.

I took my way back to the life amongst mankind, my brothers and equals—in all the souls of whom dwells Tao, primordial and eternal.

The ornamental lights of the harbour gleamed already in the distance, and the drone of the great town sounded nearer and nearer to us over the sea.

Then I felt a great strength in me, and I ordered the boatman to row still more quickly. I was ready. Was I not as safely and well cared for in the great town as in the still country?—in in the street as on the sea?

In everything, everywhere, dwells Poetry—Love—Tao. And the whole world is a great sanctuary, as well-devised and surely maintained as a strong, well-ordered house.

"We fit as naturally into this beauty around us as a tree or a mountain. If we can but remain so always, we shall retain the feeling of our own well-being amid all the great workings of the world-system. So much has always been said about human life; and scholars have created such an endless labyrinth of theories! And yet in its inmost kernel it is as plain as nature. All things are equal in simplicity, and nothing is really in confusion, however much it may seem as though it were so. Everything moves surely and inevitably as the sea. It is all a manifestation of divine love,—Tao is the Spirit of God in the world."

STORY OF EFFORT AND DESTINY

Told by

LANG LI FU

Effort said to Destiny:

"Your achievements are not equal to mine."

"Pray what do you achieve in the working of things," replied Destiny, "that you would compare yourself with me?" "Why," said Effort, "the length of man's life, his measure of success, his rank, and his wealth, are all things which I have the power to determine." To this, Destiny made reply: "P'eng Tsu'n wisdom did not exceed that of Yao and Shun, yet he lived to the age of eight hundred. Yen Yuan's ability was not inferior to that of the average man, yet he died at the early age of thirty-two. The virtue of Confucius was not less than that of the feudal princes, yet he was reduced to sore straits between Ch'en and Ts'ai.

"The conduct of Chou, of the Yin dynasty, did not surpass that of the Three Men of Virtue, yet he occupied a kingly throne.

"Chi Cha would not accept the overlordship of wu, while T'ien Heng usurped sole power in Ch'i.

Po I and Shu Ch'i starved to death at Shou-yang, while Chi Shih waxed rich at Chan-Ch'in. If these results were compassed by your efforts, how is it that you allotted long life to P'eng Tsu and an untimely death to Yen Yuan; that you awarded discomfiture to the sage and success to the impious, humiliation to the wise man and high honours to the fool, poverty to the good and wealth to the wicked?" "If, as you say," rejoined Effort, "I have really no control over events, is it not, then, owing to your management that things turn out as they do?" Destiny replied: "The very name 'Destiny' (Something already immutably fixed) shows that there can be no question of management in the case. When the way is straight, I push on; when it is crooked, I let be. Old age and early death, failure and success, high rank and humble station, riches and poverty—all these come naturally and of themselves. Of their ultimate causes, I am ignorant; how could it be otherwise?

"Being what it is, without knowing why—that is the meaning of Destiny. What room is there for management here?"

THE ILLNESS OF CHI LIANG
Told by
MING HI

Yang Chu had a friend called Chi Liang, who fell ill. In seven days' time his illness had become very grave; medical aid was summoned, and his sons stood weeping round his bed. Chi Liang said to Yang Chu: "Such excess of emotion shows my children to be degenerate. Will you kindly sing them something that will enlighten their minds?" Yang Chu then chanted the following words:

"How should men possess the knowledge which God Himself has not? Over his destiny man has no control, and can look for no help from God. You and I know this for truth, but our knowledge is not shared by sorcerers and quacks."

The sons, however, did not understand, and finally called in three physicians, Dr. Chiao, Dr. Yü and Dr. Lu. They all diagnosed his complaint; and Dr. Chiao delivered his opinion first: "The hot and cold elements of your body," he said to Chi Liang, "are not in harmonious accord, and the impermeable and infundibular parts are natually disproportionate. The origin of your malady is traceable to disordered appetites, and to the dissipation of your vital essence through worry and care. Neither God nor devil is to blame. Although the illness is grave, it is amenable to treatment." Chi Liang said: "You are only one of the common ruck," and speedily got rid of him. Then Dr. Yü came forward and said: "You were born with too little nervous force, and were too freely fed with mother's milk. Your illness is not one that has developed in a matter of twenty-four hours; the causes which have led up to it are of general growth. It is incurable." Chi Liang replied: "You are a good doctor," and told them to give him some food. Lastly, Dr. Lu said: "Your illness is attributable neither to God, nor to man, nor to the agency of spirits. It was already fore-ordained in the mind of Providence when you were endowed with this bodily form at birth. What possible good can herbs and drugs do you?" "You are a heaven-born physician indeed!" cried Chi Liang; and he sent him away laden with presents.

Not long after, his illness disappeared of itself.

———

Duke Ching of Ch'i was travelling across the northern flank of the Ox-mountain in the direction of the capital. Gazing at the view before him, he burst into a flood of tears, exclaiming: "What a lovely scene! How verdant and luxuriantly wooded! To think that some day I must die and leave my kingdom, passing away like running water! If only there were no such thing as death, nothing should induce me to stir from this spot." Two of the Ministers in attendance on the Duke, taking the cue from him, also began to weep, saying: "We, who are dependent on your Highness' bounty, whose food is of an inferior sort, who have to ride on unbroken horses or in jolting carts—even we do not want to die. How much less our sovereign liege!"

Yen Tzu, meanwhile, was standing by, with a broad smile on his face. The Duke wiped away his tears and, looking at him, said: "Today I am stricken with grief on my journey, and both K'ung and Chu mingle their tears with mine. How is it that you alone can smile?" Yen Tzu replied: "If the worthy ruler were to remain in perpetual possession of his realm, Duke T'ai and Duke Huan would still be exercising their sway. If the bold ruler were to remain in perpetual possession, Duke Chuang and Duke Ling would still be ruling the land. But if all these rulers were now in possession, where would your Highness be? Why, standing in the furrowed fields, clad in coir cape and hat! Condemned to a hard life on earth, you would have had no time, I warrant, for brooding over death. Again, how did you yourself come to occupy this throne? By a series of successive reigns and removals, until at last your turn came. And are you alone going to weep and lament over this order of things? That is unmanly. It was the sight of these two objects—an unmanly prince and his fawning attendants—that was affording me food for laughter just now."

Duke Ching felt much ashamed and, raising his goblet, fined himself and his obsequious courtiers two cups of wine apiece.

THE INTELLIGENCE OF ANIMALS

Told by

YIN HSI

When the Yellow Emperor fought with Yen Ti on the field of P'an-ch'uan, his vanguard was composed of bears, wolves, panthers, lynxes and tigers, while his ensign-bearers were eagles, ospreys, falcons and kites. This was forcible im-

pressment of animals into the service of man.
The Emperor Yao entrusted K'uei with the reg-
ulation of the music. And when he tapped the
musical stone in varying cadence, all the animals
danced to the sound of the music. When the
strains of the Shao were heard on the flute, the
phoenix itself flew down to assist. This was the
attraction of animals by the power of music. In
what, then, do the minds of birds and beasts differ
from the minds of men? Only the sounds they
utter are different, and the secret by which com-
munication may be effected is unknown. But
the wisdom and penetration of the Sage are un-
limited: that is why he is able to lead them to do
his bidding. The intelligence of animals is in-
nate even as that of man. Their common desire
is for propagation of life, but their instincts are
not derived from any human source. There is
pairing between the male and the female, and
mutual attachment between the mother and her
young. They shun the open plain and keep to
the mountainous parts; they flee the cold and
make for warmth; when they settle, they gather
in flocks: when they travel, they preserve a fixed
order. The young ones are stationed in the middle, the stronger ones place themselves on the
outside. They show one another the way to the

drinking-places, and call to their fellows when there is food. In the earliest ages, they dwelt and moved about in company with man. It was not until the age of emperors and kings that they began to be afraid and broke away into scattered bands. And now, in this final period, they habitually hide and keep out of man's way so as to avoid injury at his hands. At the present day, the Chieh-shih people in the Far East can in many cases interpret the language of the six domestic animals, although they have probably but an imperfect understanding of it.

In remote antiquity, there were men of divine enlightenment who were perfectly acquainted with the feelings and habits of all living things, and thoroughly understood the language of the various species. The latter assembled at their bidding, and received the instruction imparted to them, exactly like human beings. . . . These sages declared that, in mind and understanding, there was no wide gulf between any of the living species endowed with blood and breath. And, therefore, knowing that this was so, they neglected or passed over none that came to them for instruction.

A BAD MEMORY

Told by

KUAN TZU

Yang-li-Hua-tzu, of the Sung State, was afflicted in middle age by the disease of amnesia. Anything he received in the morning he had forgotten by the evening; anything he gave away in the evening he had forgotten the next morning. Out-of-doors, he forgot to talk; indoors, he forgot to sit down. At any given moment, he had no recollection of what had just taken place; and a little later on, he could not even recollect what had happened then. All his family were perfectly disgusted with him. Fortune-tellers were summoned, but their divinations proved unsuccessful; wizards were sought out, but their exorcisms were ineffectual; physicians were called in, but their remedies were of no avail. At last, a learned professor from the Lu State volunteered his services, declaring that he could effect a cure. Hua-tzu's wife and family immediately offered him half their landed property if only he would tell them how to set to work. The professor replied: "This is a case which cannot be dealt with by means of auspices and diagrams;

the evil cannot be removed by prayers and in·
cantations, nor successfully combated by drugs
and potions. What I shall try to do is to influence his mind and turn the current of his
thoughts; in that way cure is likely to be brought
about."

Accordingly, the experiment was begun. The
professor exposed his patient to cold, so that he
was forced to beg for clothes; subjected him to
hunger, so that he was fain to ask for food; left
him in darkness, so that he was obliged to search
for light. Soon, he was able to report progress
to the sons of the house, saying gleefully: "The
disease can be checked. But the methods I shall
employ have been handed down as a secret in
my family, and cannot be made known to the
public. All attendants must, therefore, be dismissed, and I must be shut up alone with my
patient." The professor was allowed to have
his way, and for the space of seven days no one
knew what was going on in the sick man's chamber. Then, one fine morning, the treatment
came to an end, and, wonderful to relate, the
disease of so many years' standing had entirely
disappeared!

No sooner had Hua-tzu regained his senses,
however, than he flew into a great rage, drove

A CHINESE MOTHER TELLING FAIRY TALES

his wife out-of-doors, beat his sons, and, snatching up a spear, hotly pursued the professor through the town. On being arrested and asked to explain his conduct, this is what he said: "Lately, when I was steeped in forgetfulness, my senses were so benumbed that I was quite unconscious of the existence of the outer world. But now I have been brought suddenly to a perception of the events of a lifetime. Preservation and destruction, gain and loss, sorrow and joy, love and hate have begun to throw out their myriad tentacles to invade my peace; and these emotions will, I fear, continue to keep my mind in the state of turmoil that I now experience. Oh! if I could but recapture a short moment of that blessed oblivion!"

THE DREAMS OF KAN YIN

Told by

HEN TSUNG

Kan Yin of Chou was the owner of a large estate, who harried his servants unmercifully, and gave them no rest from morning to night. There was one old servant in particular whose physical strength had quite left him; yet his master worked him all the harder. All day

long he was groaning as he went about his work,
and when night came he was reeling with fatigue
and would sleep like a log. His spirit was then
free to wander at will, and every night be dreamt
that he was a king, enthroned in authority over
the multitude, and controlling the affairs of the
whole State. He took his pleasure in palaces
and belvederes, following his own fancy in everything, and his happiness was beyond compare.
But when he awoke, he was a servant once more.
To some one who condoled with him on his hard
lot the old man replied: "Human life may last
a hundred years, and the whole of it is equally
divided into nights and days. In the daytime I
am only a slave, it is true, and my misery cannot
be gainsaid. But by night I am a king, and my
happiness is beyond compare. So what have I
to grumble at?"

Now, Kan Yin's mind was full of wordly cares,
and he was always thinking with anxious solici-
tude about the affairs of his estate. Thus he was
wearing out mind and body alike, and at night he
also used to fall asleep utterly exhausted. Every
night he dreamt that he was another man's servant, running about on menial business of every
discription, and subjected to every possible kind
of abuse and ill-treatment. He would mutter

and groan in his sleep, and obtained no relief until morning came. This state of things at last resulted in a serious illness, and Mr. Yin besought the advice of a friend. "Your station in life," his friend said, "is a distinguished one, and you have wealth and property in abundance. In these respects you are far above the average. If at night you dream that you are a servant and exchange ease for affliction, that is only the proper balance in human destiny. What you want is that your dreams should be as pleasant as your waking moments. But that is beyond your power to compass." On hearing what his friend said, Mr. Yin lightened his servant's toil and allowed his own mental worry to abate; whereupon his malady began to decrease in proportion.

THE WOOD GATHERER

Told by

TAN FAN FU

A man was gathering fuel in the Cheng State when he fell in with a deer that had been startled from its usual haunts. He gave chase, and succeeded in killing it. He was overjoyed at his good luck; but, for fear of discovery, he hastily concealed the carcass in a dry ditch, and covered it up with brushwood. Afterwards, he forgot the spot where he had hidden the deer, and finally became convinced that the whole affair was only a dream. He told the story to people as he went along; and one of those who heard it, following the indications given, went and found the deer. On reaching home with his booty, this man made the following statement to his wife: "Once upon a time," he said, "a woodcutter dreamt that he had got a deer, but coudn't remember the place where he had put it. Now I have found the deer, so it appears that his dream was a true dream." "On the contrary," said his wife, "it is you who must have dreamt that you met a wood-cutter who had caught the deer. Here you have a deer, true enough. But where is the wood-cutter? It is evidently your dream that has come true." "I have certainly got a deer," replied her husband; "so what does it matter to us whether it was his dream or mine?"

Meanwhile, the woodcutter had gone home, not at all disgusted at having lost the deer. For he thought the whole thing must have been a dream. But the same night, he saw in a dream the place where he had really hidden it, and he also dreamt of the man who had taken it. So, the next morning in accordance with his dream, he went to seek him out in order to recover the deer. A quarrel ensued, and the matter was finally brought before the magistrate, who gave judgment in these terms: "You," he said to the woodcutter, "began by really killing a deer, but wrongly thought it was a dream. Then you really dreamt that you had got the deer, but wrongly took the dream to be reality. The other man really took your deer, which he is now disputing with you. His wife, on the other hand, declares that she saw both men and deer in a dream, so that nobody can be said to have killed the deer at all. Meanwhile, here is the deer itself in court, and you had better divide it between you."

The case was reported to the Prince of the Cheng State, who said: "Why, the magistrate must have dreamt the whole thing himself!" The question was referred to the Prime Minister, but the latter confessed himself unable to disentangle the part that was a dream from the part that was not a dream. "If you want to distinguish between waking and dreaming," he said, "you would have to go back to the Yellow Emperor or Confucius. But both these sages are dead, and there is nobody now alive who can draw any such distinction."

THE JOURNEY OF LIFE

Told by

YÜ HSIUNG, *the Taoist Sage*

The ancients spoke of the dead as kuei-jen (men who have returned). But if the dead are men who have returned, the living are men on a journey. Those who are on a journey and think not of returning have cut themselves off from their home. Should any one man cut himself off from his home, he would incur universal reprobation. But all mankind being homeless, there is none to see the error. Imagine one who leaves his native village, separates himself from all his kith and kin, dissipates his patrimony and wanders away to the four corners of the earth, never to return:—what manner of man is this? The world will surely set him down as a profligate and a vagabond. On the other hand, imagine one who clings to respectability and the things of this life, holds cleverness and capacity in high esteem, builds himself up a reputation, and plays the braggart amongst his fellow men without knowing where to stop:—what manner of man, once more, is this? The world will surely look upon him as a gentleman of great wisdom and counsel. Both of these men have lost their way, yet the world will consort with the one, and not with the other. Only the Sage knows with whom to consort and from whom to hold aloof."

ON EVOLUTION
Told by
YÜ HSIUNG, *the Taoist Sage*

Yü Hsiung said: "Evolution is never-ending. But who can perceive the secret processes of Heaven and Earth? Thus, things that are diminished here are augmented there; things that are made whole in one place suffer loss in another. Diminution and augmentation, fullness and decay are the constant accompaniments of life and death. They alterate in continuous succession, and we are not conscious of any interval. The whole body of spiritual substance progresses without a pause; the whole body of material substance suffers decay without intermission. But we do not perceive the process of completion, nor do we perceive the process of decay. Man, likewise, from birth to old age becomes something different every day in face and form, in wisdom and in conduct. His skin, his nails and his hair are continually growing and continually perishing. In infancy and child-hood there is no stopping nor respite from change. Though inperceptible while it is going on, it may be verified afterwards if we wait."

MAN AND THE UNIVERSE

Told by

YÜ HSIUNG, *the Taoist Sage*

There was once a man in the Ch'i State who was so afraid the universe would collapse and fall to pieces leaving his body without lodgment, that he could neither sleep nor eat. Another man, pitying his distress, went to enlighten him. "Heaven," he said, "is nothing more than an ac-cumulation of ether, and there is no place where ether is not. Processes of contraction and ex-pansion, inspiration and expiration are contin-ually taking place up in the heavens. Why then should you be afraid of a collapse?" The man said: "It is true that Heaven in an ac-cumulation of ether; but the sun, the moon, and the stars—will they not fall down upon us?" His informant replied: "Sun, moon and stars are likewise only bright lights within this mass of ether. Even supposing they were to fall, they could not possibly harm us by their impact." "But what if the earth should fall to pieces?" "The earth," replied the other, "is merely an agglomeration of matter, which fills and blocks up the four corners of space. There is no part of it where matter is not. All day long there is constant treading and tramping on the surface of the earth. Why then should you be afraid of its falling to pieces?" Thereupon the man was relieved of his fears and rejoiced exceedingly. And his instructor was also joyful and easy in mind. But Ch'ang Lu Tzu laughed at them both, saying: "Rainbows, clouds and mist, wind and rain, the four seasons—these are perfected forms of accumulated ether, and go to make up the heavens. Mountains and cliffs, rivers and seas, metals and rocks, fire and timber —these are perfected forms of agglomerated matter, and constitute the earth. Knowing these facts, who can say that they will never be destroyed? Heaven and earth form only a small speck in the midst of the Void, but they are the greatest things in the sun of Being. This much is certain: even as their nature is hard to fathom, hard to understand, so they will be slow to pass away, slow to come to an end. He who fears lest they should suddenly fall to pieces is assuredly very far from the truth. He, on the other hand, who says that they will never be destroyed has also not reached the right solution. Heaven and earth must of necessity pass away, but neither will revert to destruction apart from the other. Who, having to face the day of disruption, would not be alarmed?"

The Master Lieh Tzu (a disciple of Lao Tzu), heard of discussion, and smiling said: "He who maintains that Heaven and earth are destructible, and he who upholds the contrary, are both equally at fault. Whether they are destructible or not is something we can never know, though one may hold this view and another that. The living and the dead, the going and the coming, know nothing of each other's state. Whether destruction awaits the world or no, why should I trouble my head about it?"

DREAMS

Told by

YÜ HSIUNG, *the Taoist Sage*

In the time of King Mu of Chou, there was a magician who came from a kingdom in the far west. He could pass through fire and water, penetrate metal and stone, overturn mountains and make rivers flow backwards, transplant whole towns and cities, ride on thin air without

falling, encounter solid bodies without being ob-
structed. There was no end to the countless
variety of changes and transformations which he
could effect; and besides changing the external
form, he could also spirit away men's internal
cares.

King Mu revered him as a god, and served him
like a prince. He set aside for his use a spacious
suite of apartments, regaled him with the
daintiest of food, and selected a number of sing-
ing-girls for his express gratification. The
magician, however, condemned the King's palace
as mean, the cooking as rancid, and the con-
cubines as too ugly to live with. So King Mu
had a new building errected to please him. It
was built entirely of bricks and wood, and gorge-
ously decorated in red and white, no skill being
spared in its construction. The five royal treas-
uries were empty by the time that the new pavilion was complete. It stood six thousand feet
high, overtopping Mount Chung-nan, and it was
called Touch-the-sky Pavilion. Then the King
proceeded to fill it with maidens, selected from
Cheng and Wie, of the most exquisite and delicate beauty. They were anointed with fragrant perfumes, provided with jewelled hairpins
and earrings, and arrayed in the finest silks,

with costly satin trains. Their faces were powdered, and their eyebrows pencilled, their girdles were studded with precious stones, and sweet scents were wafted abroad wherever they went. Ravishing music was played to the honoured guest by the Imperial bands; several times a month he was presented with fresh jewelled raiment; every day he had set before him some new and delicious food.

The magician could not well refuse to take up his abode in this palace of delight. But he had not dwelt there very long when he invited the King to accompany him on a jaunt. So the king clutched the magician's sleeve, and soared up with him higher and higher into the sky, until at last they stopped, and lo! they had reached the magician's own palace. This palace was built with beams of gold and silver, and incrusted with pearls and jade. It towered high above the region of clouds and rain, and the foundations whereon it rested were unknown. It appeared like a stupendous cloud-mass to the view. The sights and sounds it offered to eye and ear, the scents and flavours which abounded there, were such as exist not within mortal ken. The King verily believed that he was in the Halls of Paradise, tenanted by God himself, and that he was

listening to the mighty music of the spheres. He
gazed at his own palace on the earth below, and
it seemed to him no better than a rude pile of
clods and brushwood.

The King would gladly have stayed in this
palace for decade after decade, without a thought
for his own country. But the magician invited
him to make another journey, and in the new region they came to, neither sun nor moon could be
seen in the heavens above, nor any rivers or seas
below. The King's eyes were dazed by the qual-
ity of the light, and he lost the power of vision;
his ears were stunned by the sounds that assailed
them, and he lost the faculty of hearing. The
framework of his bones and his internal organs
were thrown out of gear and refused to function.
His thoughts were in a whirl, his intellect became
clouded, and he begged the magician to take him
back again. Thereupon, the magician gave him
a shove, and the King experienced a sensation of
falling through space. . . .

When he awoke to consciousness, he found
himself sitting on his throne just as before, with
the selfsame attendants round him. He looked
at the wine in front of him, and saw that
it was still full of sediment; he looked at
the viands, and found that they had not yet

lost their freshness. He asked where he had come from, and his attendants told him that he had only been sitting quietly there. This threw King Mu into a reverie, and it was three months before he was himself again. Then he made further inquiry, and asked the magician to explain what had happened. "Your Majesty and I," replied the magician, "were only wandering about in the spirit, and, of course, our bodies never moved at all. What essential difference is there between that sky-palace we dwelt in and your Majesty's palace on earth, between the spaces we travelled through and your Majesty's own park?

During your retirement from public affairs, you have been in a perpetual state of doubt as to the reality of your experience. But in a universe where changes are everlastingly in progress, and fast and slow are purely relative conceptions, how can the Ideal ever be fully attained?"

A TAOIST CHARLATAN

Told by

YÜ HSIUNG, the Taoist Sage

Mr. Fan had a son named Tzu Hua, who succeeded in achieving great fame as an exponent of the black art, and the whole kingdom bowed down before him. He was in high favour with the Prince of Chin, taking no office but standing on a par with the three Ministers of State. Any one on whom he turned a partial eye was marked out for distinction; while those of whom he spoke unfavourably were forthwith banished. People thronged his hall in the same way as they went to Court. Tzu Hua used to encourage his followers to contend amongst themselves, so that the clever ones were always bullying the slow-witted, and the strong riding rough-shod over the weak. Though this resulted in blows and wounds being dealt before his eyes, he was not in the habit of troubling about it. Day and night, this sort of thing served as an amusement, and practically became a custom in the State.

One day, Ho Sheng and Tzu Po, two of Fan's leading disciples, set off on a journey and, after traversing a stretch of wild country, they put up for the night in the hut of an old peasant named Shang Ch'iu K'ai. During the night, the two travellers conversed together, speaking of Tzu Hua's reputation and influence, his power over the fortunes of others, and how he could make the rich man poor and the poor man rich. Now, Shang Ch'iu K'ai was living on the border of starvation. He had crept round under the window and overheard this conversation. Accordingly, he borrowed some provisions and, shouldering his basket, set off for Tzu Hua's establishment. This man's followers, however, were a worldly set, who wore silken garments and rode in high carriages and stalked about with their noses in the air. Seeing that Shang Ch'iu K'ai was advanced in years and deficient in strength, with a weather-beaten face and clothes of no particular cut, they one and all despised him. Soon he became a regular target for their insults and ridicule, being hustled about and slapped on the back and what not. Shang Ch'iu K'ai, however, never showed the least annoyance, and at last the disciples, having exhausted their wit on him in this way, grew tired of the fun. So, by way of a jest, they took the old man with them to the top of a cliff, and word was passed round that whosoever dared to throw himself over would be rewarded with a hundred ounces of silver. There was an eager response, and Shang Ch'iu K'ai, in perfect good faith, was the first to leap over the edge. And lo! he was wafted down to earth like a bird on the wing, not a bone or muscle of his body being hurt. Mr. Fan's disciples, regarding this as a lucky chance, were merely surprised, but not yet moved to great wonder. Then they pointed to a bend in the foaming river below, saying: "There is a precious pearl at the bottom of that river, which can be had for the diving." Shang Ch'iu K'ai again acted on their suggestion and plunged in. And when he came out, sure enough he held a pearl in his hand.

Then, at last, the whole company began to suspect the truth, and Tzu Hua gave orders that an array of costly viands and silken raiment should be prepared; then suddenly a great fire was kindled round the pile. "If you can walk through the midst of these flames," he said, "you are welcome to keep what you can get of these embroidered stuffs, be it much or little, as a reward." Without moving a muscle of his face, Shang Ch'iu K'ai walked straight into the fire, and came back again with his garments unsoiled and his body unsinged.

Mr. Fan and his disciples now realized that he was in possession of Tao, and all began to make their apologies, saying: "We did not know, Sir, that you had Tao, and were only playing a trick on you. We insulted you, not knowing that you were a divine man. You have exposed our stupidity, our deafness and our blindness. May we

venture to ask what the Great Secret is?" "Secret I have none," replied Shang Ch'iu K'ai.
"Even in my own mind I have no clue as to the
real cause. Nevertheless, there is one point in
it all which I must try to explain to you. A
short time ago, Sir, two disciples of yours came
and put up for the night in my hut. I heard
them extolling the power of Mr. Fan, and how he
was able to make or mar people's fortunes, making the rich man poor and the poor man rich.
I believed this implicitly, and as the distance was
not very great I came hither. Having arrived,
I unreservedly accepted as true all the state-
ments made by your disciples, and was only
afraid lest the opportunity might never come of
putting them triumphantly to the proof. I knew
not what part of space my body occupied, nor
yet where danger lurked. My mind was simply
One, and material objects thus offered no resis-
tance. That is all. But now, having discovered
that your disciples were deceiving me, my inner
man is thrown into a state of doubt and perplex-
ity, while outwardly my senses of sight and hearing re-assert themselves. When I reflect I have
just had a providential escape from being
drowned and burned to death, my heart within
me freezes with horror, and my limbs tremble

with fear. I shall never again have the courage to go near water or fire."

From that time forth, when Mr. Fan's disciples happened to meet a beggar or a poor horse-doctor on the road, so far from jeering at him, they would actually dismount and offer him a humble salute.

Tsai Wo heard this story, and told it to Confucius. "Is this so strange to you?" was the reply. "The man of perfect faith can extend his influence to inanimate things and disembodied spirits; he can move heaven and earth, and fly to the six cardinal points without encountering any hindrance. His powers are not confined to walking in perilous places and passing through water and fire. If Shang Ch'iu K'ai, whose belief was false, found no obstacle in external matter, how much more certainly will that be so when both parties are equally sincere. Young man, bear this in mind."

THE TAOIST KEEPER

Told by

YÜ HSIUNG, the Taoist Sage

The Keeper of Animals under King Hsuan, of the Chou dynasty, had an assistant named

Liang Yang, who was skilled in the management of wild birds and beasts. When he fed them in their park-enclosure, all the animals showed themselves tame and tractable, although they comprised tigers, wolves, eagles, and ospreys. Male and female freely propagated their kind, and their numbers multiplied. The different species lived promiscuously together, yet they never clawed nor bit one another.

The King was afraid lest this man's secret should die with him, and commanded him to impart it to the Keeper. So Liang Yang appeared before the Keeper and said: "I am only a humble servant, and have really nothing to impart. I fear the King has been leading you to expect some mysterious secret. With regard to my method of feeding tigers, all I have to say is this: when yielded to, they are pleased; when opposed they are angry. Such is the national disposition of all living creatures. But neither their pleasure nor their anger is manifested without a cause. Both are really excited by opposition. Anger directly, pleasure indirectly, owing to the natural reaction when the opposition is overcome.

"In feeding tigers, then, I avoid giving them either live animals or whole carcasses, lest in the former case the act of killing, in the latter case the act of tearing them to pieces, should excite them to fury. Again, I time their periods of hunger and repletion, and I gain a full understanding of the causes of their anger. Tigers are of a different species from man, but, like him, they are docile with those who treat them kindly, though they will show fight when their lives are attacked. But I do not think of opposing them and thus provoking their anger; neither do I humour them and thus cause them to feel pleased. For this feeling of pleasure will in time be succeeded by anger, just as anger must invariably be succeeded by pleasure. Neither of these states hits the proper mean. Hence it is my aim to be neither antagonistic nor compliant, so that the animals regard me as one of themselves. Thus it happens that they walk about the park without regretting the tall forests and the broad marches, and rest in the enclosure without yearning for the lonely mountains and the dark valleys. Such is the effect of using one's common sense."

THE DONKEY'S REVENGE
Told by
KAI LI KUNG

Chung Ch'ing-yu was a scholar of some reputation, who lived in Manchuria. When he went up for his master's degree, he heard that there was a Taoist priest at the capital who would tell people's fortunes, and was very anxious to see him; and at the conclusion of the second part of the examination, he accidentally met him at Paot'u-ch'uan. The priest was over sixty years of age, and had the usual white beard flowing down over his breast. Around him stood a perfect wall of people inquiring their future fortunes, and to each the old man made a brief reply: but when he saw Chung among the crowd, he was overjoyed, and seizing him by the hand, said, "Sir, your virtuous intentions command my esteem." He then led him up behind a screen, and asked if he did not wish to know what was to come; and when Chung replied in the affirmative, the priest informed him that his prospects were bad. "You may succeed in passing this examination," continued he, "but on your returning covered with honour to your home, I fear that your mother will be no longer there." Now

Chung was a very filial son; and as soon as he heard these words, his tears began to flow, and he declared that he would go back without competing any further. The priest observed that if he let this chance slip, he could never hope to have her back again, and that even the rank of Viceroy would not repay him for her loss. "Well," said the priest, "you and I were connected in a former existence, and I must do my best to help you now." So he took out a pill which he gave to Chung, and told him that if he sent it post-haste by some one to his mother, it would prolong her life for seven days, and thus he would be able to see her once again after the examination was over. Chung took the pill, and went off in very low spirits; but he soon reflected that the span of human life is a matter of destiny, and that every day he could spend at home would be one more day devoted to the service of his mother. Accordingly, he got ready to start at once, and, hiring a donkey, actually set out on his way back. When he had gone about half-a-mile, the donkey turned round and ran home; and when he used his whip, the animal threw itself down on the ground. Chung got into a great perspiration, and his servant recommended him to remain where he was; but this he would not hear of, and hired another donkey, which served him exactly the same trick as the other one. The sun was now sinking behind the hills, and his servant advised his master to stay and finish his examination while he himself went back home before him. Chung had no alternative but to assent, and the next day he hurried through with his papers, starting immediately afterwards, and not stopping at all on the way either to eat or to sleep. All night long he went on, and arrived to find his mother in a very critical state; however, when he gave her the pill she so far recovered that he was able to go in to see her. Grasping his hand, she begged him not to weep, telling him that she had just dreamt she had been down to the Infernal Regions, where the King of Hell had informed her with a gracious smile that her record was fairly clean, and that in view of the filial piety of her son she was to have twelve more years of life. Chung rejoiced at this, and his mother was soon restored to her former health.

Before long the news arrived that Chung had passed his examinations; upon which he bade adieu to his mother, and went off to the capital, where he bribed the eunuchs of the palace to communicate with his friend the Taoist priest. The latter was very much pleased, and came out to see him, whereupon Chung prostrated himself at his feet. "Ah," said the priest, "this success of yours, and the prolongation of your good mother's life, is all a reward for your virtuous conduct. What have I done in the matter?" Chung was very much astonished that the priest should already know what had happened; however, he now inquired as to his own future. "You will never rise to high rank," replied the priest, "but you will attain the years of an octogenarian. In a former state of existence you and I were once traveling together, when you threw a stone at a dog, and accidentally killed a frog. Now that frog has reappeared in life as a donkey, and according to all principles of destiny you ought to suffer for what you did; but your filial piety has touched the Gods, a protecting star-influence has passed into your nativity sheet, and you will come to no harm. On the other hand, there is your wife; in her former state she was not as virtuous as she might have been, and her punishment in this life was to be widowed quite young; you, however, have secured the prolongation of your own term of years, and therefore I fear that before long your wife will pay the penalty of death." Chung was much grieved at hearing this; but after a while he asked the priest where his second wife to be was living. "At Chung-chou," replied the latter; "she is now fourteen years old." The priest then bade him adieu, telling him that if any mischance should befall him he was to hurry off towards the south-east. About a year after this, Chung's wife did die; and his mother then desiring him to go and visit his uncle, who was a magistrate in Kiangsi, on which journey he would have to pass through Chung-chou, it seemed like a fulfilment of the old priest's prophecy. As he went along, he came to a village on the banks of a river, where a large crowd of people was gathered together round a theatrical performance which was going on there. Chung would have passed quietly by, had not a stray donkey followed so close behind him that he turned round and hit it over the ears. This startled the donkey so much that it ran off full gallop, and knocked a rich gentleman's child, who was sitting with its nurse on the bank, right into the water, before any one of the servants could lend a hand to save it. Immediately there was a great outcry against Chung, who gave his mule the rein and dashed away, mindful of the priest's warning, towards the south-east. After riding about seven miles, he reached a mountain village where he saw an old man standing at the door of a house, and, jumping off his mule, made him a low bow. The old man asked him in, and inquired his name and whence he came; to which Chung replied by telling him the whole adventure. "Never fear," said the old man; "you can stay here, while I send out to learn the position of affairs." By the evening his messenger had returned, and then they knew for the first time that the child belonged to a wealthy family. The old man looked grave and said, "Had it been anybody else's child, I might have helped you; as it is I can do nothing." Chung was greatly alarmed at this; however, the old man told him to remain quietly there for the night, and see what turn matters might take. Chung was overwhelmed with anxiety, and did not sleep a wink; and next morning he heard the constables were after him, and that it was death to any one who should conceal him. The old man changed countenance at this, and went inside, leaving Chung to his own reflection; but towards the middle of the night he came and knocked at Chung's door, and, sitting down, began to ask how old his wife was. Chung replied that he was a widower; at which the old man seemed rather pleased, and declared that in such case help would be forthcoming; "for," said he, "my sister's husband has taken the vows, and become a priest, and my sister herself has died, leaving an orphan girl who has now no home; and if you would only marry her—" Chung was delighted, more especially as this would be both the fulfilment of the Taoist priest's prophecy and a means of extricating himself from his present difficulty; at the same time, he declared he should be sorry to implicate his future father-in-law. "Never mind about that," replied the old man; "sister's husband is pretty skillful in the black art. He has not mixed much with the world of late; but when you are married, you can discuss the matter with my niece." So Chung married the young lady, who was sixteen years of age, and very beautiful; but whenever he looked at her he took occasion to sigh. At last she said, "I may be ugly; but you needn't be in such a hurry to let me know it;" whereupon Chung begged her pardon, and said he felt himself only too lucky to have met with such a divine creature; adding that he sighed because he feared some misfortune was coming on them which would separate them for ever. He then told her his story, and the young lady was very angry that she should have been drawn into such a difficulty without a word of warning. Chung fell on his knees, said he had already consulted with her uncle, who was unable himself to do anything, much as he wished it. He continued that he was aware of her power; and then, pointing out that his alliance was not altogether beneath her, made all kinds of promises if she would only help him out of this trouble. The young lady was no longer able to refuse, but informed him that to apply to her father would entail certain disagreeable consequences, as he had retired from the world, and did not any more recognise her as his daughter. That night they did not attempt to sleep, spending the interval in padding their knees with thick felt concealed beneath their clothes; and then they got into chairs and were carried off to the hills. After journeying some distance, they were compelled by the nature of the road to alight and walk; and it was only by a great effort that Chung succeeded at last in getting his wife to the top. At the door of the temple they sat down to rest, the powder and paint on the young lady's face having all mixed with the perspiration trickling down; but when Chung began to apologise for bringing her to this pass, she replied that it was a mere trifle compared with what was to come. By-and-by, they went inside; and treading their way to the wall behind, found the young lady's father sitting in contem-

plation, his eyes closed, and a servant-boy standing by with a Tao Emblem. Everything was
beautifully clean and nice, but before the dais
were sharp stones scattered about as thick as the
stars in the sky. The young lady did not venture to select a favourable spot; she fell on her
knees at once, and Chung did likewise behind her.
Then the father opened his eyes, shutting them
again almost instantaneously; whereupon the
young lady said, "For a long time I have not
paid my respects to you. I am now married, and
I have brought my husband to see you." A long
time passed away, and then her father opened his
eyes and said, "You're giving a great deal of
trouble," immediately relapsing into silence a-
gain. There the husband and wife remained until the stones seemed to pierce into their very
bones; but after a while the father cried out,
"Have you brought the donkey?" His daughter replied that they had not; whereupon they
were told to go and fetch it at once, which they
did, not knowing what the meaning of this order
was. After a few more days, kneeling, they suddenly heard that the murderer of the child had
been caught and beheaded, and were just con-
gratulating each other on the success of their
scheme, when a servant came in with a stick in

his hand, the top of which had been chopped off. "This stick," said the servant, "died instead of you. Bury it reverently, that the wrong done to the tree may be somewhat atoned for." Then Chung saw that at the place where the top of the stick had been chopped off there were traces of blood; he therefore buried it with the usual ceremony, and immediately set off with his wife, and returned to his own home.

PART III

Tales Told on the Eve of

THE FEAST OF LANTERNS

T HE Chinese Calendar is lunar, but its beginning is determined by the Sun. New Year falls on the first New Moon after the Sun has entered Aquarius, which will never happen before January 21, nor after February 19. The months are strictly regulated by the Moon. The first of every month is new moon and the fifteenth is full moon. New Year's is a feast of great rejoicing. It is celebrated with paper lanterns and paper dragons, which are hung up in arbors specially erected for the purpose and carried about in procession. On the fifteenth of the month, the Chinese celebrate the birthday of the "Spirit of Heaven." Among the Gods he is the chief of a trinity which is greatly respected all over China. The other two of the trinity are the "Spirit of Earth" and the "Spirit of Water." The "Spirit of Heaven" confers upon us divine blessing; the "Spirit of Water" quenches the fires of evil, and the "Spirit of Earth" pleads for us that we may be forgiven our Sins. The birthday of the "Earth Spirit" is the fifteenth of the seventh month, and the birthday of the "Water Spirit" is the tenth of the ninth month. The New Year festivities reach their height and are ended in the "Feast of Lanterns," which happens on the fifteenth of the New Moon. On this evening there is a large gathering at the home of Tzu Chien, there is an abundance of beautifully colored lanterns hung about the place and inside large quantities of sweets, special cakes, dumplings and, most valuable of all, "Good Cheer."

When the festivities are well on and the moon is high on her way, Tzu Chien calls upon one of the party to open the Story-telling.

THE EVE OF THE FEAST OF LANTERNS

The evening of the Feast of Lanterns had arrived, and the beautifully coloured lanterns were lighted all over the town. Sun Hou, the oil merchant, and his wife went forth to enjoy themselves. They permitted their domestics to accompany them, but left their unhappy daughter Liu Chin Ting to meditate at home. Unfortunate little Chin Ting! Disconsolate little Chin Ting! She had been haunted for months past, awake and asleep, with visions of the Feast of Lanterns—the holiday of the year. The rest of the twelve moons had passed away in the dullest

monotony, and gave her a keen appetite for a
little taste of amusement. She had long been
reckoning with confidence upon this; she had
looked to the Feast of Lanterns as an occasion of
perfect felicity. She had behaved with the most
dutiful attention to her parents; they had hitherto appeared perfectly willing that she should
accompany them on that evening; she had no idea
that there could be any other object in attending
such a festival except enjoyment, or, as she called
it, fun; she had congratulated herself in the
morning that the day was so fine; and she had
anticipated abundance of fun in the evening.
Oh, must not then the disappointment of Chin
Ting have been exceeding bitter, as the goodly
fabric which hope had reared for her of all the
prettiest cards in the pack, was thus blown down
by the breath of an unkind father?

With vain entreaties she followed her parents
to the street door: they went out, closed it, and
removed the key, leaving her only one dull lantern to console her for the loss of the illumination.

She leaned against the cruel portal and sobbed
as though her little heart would have split into a
thousand pieces. "Well, this is no fun at all,"
she cried; "there's no fun for me!"

"That's as you please," observed a little voice

somewhere; but Chin Ting could not for a while discover from whence the little voice proceeded. She was startled and terrified, and glanced round without perceiving any one. At last her eye fell upon a large jar, which stood in one corner of the hall; and her astonishment was great at observing a small, round head appearing above the neck of this earthern vessel, the lid of which was raised, and served as a cap to the small round head.

Chin Ting's heart beat fast when she noticed this apparition, and she almost sank upon the ground with fright; but she kept her eyes upon the small round head, and the very good-humoured and waggish expression of the face a little reassured her.

"Don't be frightened, most beautiful Chin Ting," said the good-natured little apparition.

"I wouldn't if I could help it," stammered Chin Ting; "but who are you?"

"Why," replied the head, "I am just what you didn't expect to meet with," and it laughed.

"He laughs like fun," said Chin Ting to herself.

"I am Fun," continued the apparition; "and very much at your service."

"Who?" asked Chin Ting.

"Fun," said he; "Fun, Fun, Fun,—nobody else but Fun;" and he looked excessively funny.

"And why came you hither?" demanded Chin Ting, who began to gain courage from the pleasing manners of Fun, and to enjoy the joke of thus unexpectedly meeting with a companion.

"I came hither to see the beautiful Chin Ting," replied he; "and, if it were in my power, somewhat to console her. If she will, Fun shall be hers for ever and a day."

"But how came you hither?" she asked, her fear somewhat returning as that question occurred to her: surely, she thought, by some supernatural means.

"Why," responded Fun, "I came here,—I got in,—I appeared,—that is to say,—I have a certain talisman—"

And here Fun hatched up a long story of as many *li* as there are between Peking and Canton. There is no occasion that we should repeat all he said, or attempt to impose upon your credulity, as he did upon Chin Ting's. It was no talisman that assisted him into the jar; we will explain to you the whole truth of the matter.

Chin Ting being, as hath been said, a damsel fair and comely, and Fun having once seen her by accident, he had entertained from that time a strong and very natural desire to have her to wife. How to obtain her, however, was a difficult question. He could find nothing in the book of Rites, that would justify his forcing himself upon the acquaintance of her father; and, as an old proverb observes, "If you cannot get over the outer wall, you will not get over the inner." But Fun consoled himself with another Chinese saying: "He that would steal fruit does not borrow the gardener's ladder;" and he set his brains at work to devise some plan whereby he might possess himself of Chin Ting, without consulting her father.

When the Feast of Lanterns drew near, it occurred to Fun that that might be a convenient as well as propitious time for effecting his object; and at first he pondered on the practicability of enticing away Chin Ting, when with her parents, she would attend the exhibitions of the evening. But a more happy idea afterwards entered his mind; and he immediately engaged in operations for the execution of this project. He wrote the letter to Sun-Hou and arraying himself as a servant, delivered it at the old gentleman's door. Whilst the domestic into whose hands he had given it was absent, he looked round for a snug place in which he might hide; and observing the large jar, and considering that it was not likely that he should be detected in that, with some little difficulty he squeezed himself in, and shut down the lid. We need not speak of the mortal fright he was in until he was "safely stowe'd," lest any one should appear in the hall; but things happened luckily, and his concealment was complete.

From within his jar, the cover of which he raised a little occasionally, as well to listen to what was going on as to obtain air, he overheard much of what passed between Sun-Hou and Chin Ting, in the neighboring apartment. He was delighted at finding that everything occurred according to his anticipations; and waited, therefore, with great patience and fortitude, in a hiding-place which would not have been agreeable, certainly, for a protracted residence.

Perhaps it may occasion surprise that in writing to Sun Hou, Fun should have given his own name; that he should have directed suspicion to himself, when it would have been so easy to have found for it a different channel. But Fun was fond of frolic, and the most impudent dog in all the Central Land. He would have considered it no sport to have put old Sun Hou on a wrong scent altogether. His object was to set him at first upon a right one, and afterwards baffle him by well-managed doublings and windings; and he would not probably have troubled himself to get married at all, had it not been for the compound extract of sport he expected from hunting and from being hunted.

"And how is it, Thousand Pieces of Gold," said Fun, "that you are not abroad this night, when all other houses are deserted?—that you are not abroad, outshining the lanterns and the moon?"

"My parents," responded Chin Ting,—and at the recollection she burst again into tears— "my parents would not allow me to go forth. My father locked me up here, and told me there grew a bamboo in the garden; and all for no better reason than because I was fond of fun."

"Cruel parents! cruel father!" exclaimed the *young audacious;* "if I were the Thousand Pieces of Gold, I would exert me somehow to spite them."

"And what could poor little I do?" asked Chin Ting. "Oh, poor little luckless I!"

"I could talk more freely," said the young gentleman, "if I were out of this jar. But I am wedged in,—I am wedged in tight!" said Fun as he struggled to get out.

He struggled to get out, but in vain. We know not how it was—he had got cramped, we suppose, by his position; but, like the weasel in the fable, he could not obtain egress at the hole by which he had entered. Thus unfortunately situated, he appealed to young Chin Ting for assistance; and this, after some hesitation, she accorded. By dint then of much struggling upon his part, and of an energetic handling of his pigtail on hers, after a time he got free to the waist; but there occurred another hitch, which all their endeavours failed to overcome. Some would have been immensely annoyed; but Fun was immensely amused. At last, by stamping violently he broke out the bottom of the jar, and thrusting his legs through regained in part his locomotive power.

It will not be necessary to detail the arguments by which he overcame the scruples of Chin Ting, and induced her to assent to an elopement with him. She was anxious to spite her papa, and no less so to see the fireworks; she was pleased with the manners of Fun, and was fond of a good joke. All these considerations, aided by the young man's eloquence, might well prevail on a youthful and inexperienced girl. So Chin Ling agreed to fly with Fun; and,—by way of carrying the jest up to its climax,—to get married.

In carrying into execution this rash resolve, it was necessary, of course, to guard against her being recognized by any in the streets. She disguised herself, therefore, as well as she was able, and covered her face with a thick veil.

Another difficulty now presented itself. They were locked in—how were they to escape?

The house was of two stories; and the upper windows were not secured. They went up stairs; the young lady assisting the youth, whose jar would otherwise have proved a sad impediment to his proceeding.

But for the inconvenient armour of porcelain in which he was arrayed, Fun could easily have leaped down from the casement; for he was active and brave. As it was, however, he was again dependent upon the lady's assistance; and exerting all her strength, more than you could have imagined could be in her slender wrists, she lowered him by his queue. When she let go, he had yet a few cubits to fall, and this perhaps was a fortunate circumstance, as the porcelain jar was thereby shattered, and he walked as freely as ever. Fun, however, was a little disappointed, as he had enjoyed the idea of stalking about in such a quaint disguise.

Fun being safely on the ground, Chin Ting, with the courage befitting a heroine, leaped into his arms. They were quite unobserved; for that part of the city was wholly deserted, the people having gone to witness a very grand display of fireworks and lanterns in a neighbouring square.

Towards that square Fun immediately conducted his prize, and a very few turnings among some narrow streets and passages brought them there. They met with none to question them on the way; for even the watch had taken holiday, deeming it quite unnecessary to keep guard in empty streets. Chin Ting, no doubt, was a little frightened, as soon as she had taken her rash leap from the window, at thinking of what she had done; and very probably wished herself again within the house; but as the door was locked, it was impossible to get back; and Fun used every argument to convince her of the propriety of their proceeding, and to keep up her spirits. It was certainly a novel situation for one who before had scarcely ever even exchanged words with a gentleman, unless related to herself; but the state of excitement in which she had been all day, first from delight, and then from disappointment and anger, had led her on to do that which in other circumstances she would have looked upon as the most heinous. But what had the greatest effect in restoring the courage and spirits of Ching Ting, was the lively scene that unfolded before her, as with her guide she approached the square.

This was bounded on three sides by houses; but, on the side opposite to the one where they had entered, was terminated by the river, in that place broad, though shallow. The streets through which they had come lay somewhat higher than the square itself, and a flight of steps led down thereinto; so that before they descended, they had a good view of the large open area, and also of the water and houses beyond. Immediately before them was a dense mass of people, every individual flourishing a lantern; festoons of lanterns were suspended above them upon poles, and likewise between the houses; the stream was overspread with boats of all sorts and sizes, the decks, the masts, and, in fact, every part covered with lamps and lanterns; and numberless pagodas and other high buildings on the further side of the river, some near, and others at a great distance, were similarly adorned with lights innumerable. From a raised platform in the middle of the square, as well as from many remoter points, a girondola of rockets was fre-

quently thrown up; and in the intervals a display was made of other fireworks of most
ingenious invention. Luminous globes rose high
in the air, and burst with showers of coloured
light, from among which soared large birds, and
winged horses and dragons, blue, yellow, green
and crimson; and these seemed to chase each
other, and again to spit forth fire in new forms.
Now and then down the river would float a huge
and stately serpent, its body drawn up in many
graceful bends—a serpent, perhaps, of emerald
light, with eyes of intense red,—and from its
mouth would drop continual balls of fire, which,
falling on the river, assumed the form of little
luminous boats, and spread far and wide upon
the surface. From myriads of people arose con-
stantly shouts of applause and laughter; and
when these for a moment were still, the more
melodious tones of musical glasses and other instruments seemed to supply a sort of magical
harmony, in keeping with the wonderful sights.

Chin Ting was bewildered and delighted.
She watched for a time the more striking and
resplendent fireworks, and was dazzled and confused by the myriads of starry lights that
studded the air all around, that sprinkled the
sky, and were reflected from the water. After a

little she began to examine the lanterns and other luminous devices in detail; they were worth examination, for their ingenuity was great, and their variety surprising. Every one had striven to outdo his neighbour in providing himself with a lantern, remarkable for its size, or for its colour, or its form, or for the designs wherewith it was embellished. There were some of all sizes, from an orange to a watch-box; of all shapes, round, square, polygonal, vase-like. like flowers, like trees, like animals, like men; of all colours, with inscriptions and paintings of all shades of colour, and ornamented with devices of the variety of which could be given but a faint idea: the current of air caused by the flame was used to set in motion small figures of men, birds, and butterflies, junks, windmills, fish, and other things and creatures; and warriors fought, and horses leaped, and mandarins bowed, and monkeys swung upon cords.

"He-he!" said Chin Ting, "see there! that tumbler standing on his head—look! look how he turns about!—and there is a mandarin with a blue body and a yellow face. Ski! hi! what a beautiful firework!—as like a peacock as two betel nuts! But, ha! he! hey! ho! hee! what is this little fellow doing? Just look! see! note!

observe! mark!—why he's dancing Djim-Kro!"

(Djim-Kro was a famous tumbler, who lived in the days of Yu.)

"Do but behold that absurd little man," said Fun, pointing in another direction, "how he waddles along, with a lantern twice as large as himself. And that ugly old woman by his side."

Chin Ting looked at the persons to whom he pointed, and immediately uttered a scream. The cause of her alarm may be easily divined. The twain were no other than her dreaded papa and mamma. She well-nigh fainted; but was supported by Fun, who reminded her that her disguise was such, as, if she would but command her fears, must render detection impossible.

Of course, Fun immediately conducted the runaway young lady to a part of the square remote from that in which they had discovered Sun Hou. No "of course" in the case. Fun did no such thing: he obtained from Chin Ting a promise that she would keep up her courage, and he immediately walked with her up to the old gentleman, her highly respectable papa.

Sun Hou was strutting with the importance of a person who knew that he was burning his own oil; he had fastened a long bamboo to his back by means of a cord round his waist; and to the end of this, which rose two or three yards above his head, was suspended his enormous lantern; his wife carried hers in the same manner, as did thousands of other persons.

Fun approached, and having made six or eight very polite bows, in returning which the old gentleman nearly shook his lantern off the end of the bamboo, our audacious young friend demanded, with the politest form of circumlocution, whether his "venerable uncle" did not rejoice in the name of Sun Hou.

"Sun Hou," replied Sun Hou with affected humility, "Sun Hou is your servant's very ignoble name."

"Methinks," said Fun, "your Humble Servant has the honour of addressing that very illustrious Sun Hou, who lives in the conspicuous corner house of the highly magnificent lane, called the Alley of the Salted Sturgeon?"

"Your servitor," answered Sun Hou, "dwells in the place you mention. May he ask your most honourable title?"

"The continually-to-be-sneezed-at name of your Humble Servant," said Fun, "is Fan-Si. I just now slunk along by your most noble dwelling, and had the little deserved honour of beholding your pile-of-volumes son, and your string-of-rubies daughter, at the window. Your Humble servant wondered greatly that they came not hither to make the lamps burn more brightly."

"Of a truth," responded Sun Hou, "had more of my oil been used, the illumination would have been more luminous. But son have I none, though I have a disobedient slip of a daughter."

"It was then perhaps your full-of-desert daughter's most profoundly-to-be-reverenced husband?"

"There was no one," replied Sun Hou, "there was no man whatever in my house: my daughter is not married. Surely your exemplary eyes must have made some mistake." But Sun Hou was startled somewhat.

"Indeed!" cried Fun: "toad as I am, I am quite certain that I beheld with my one-bigger-than-the-other eyes, two persons, a gentleman and a lady, at the window of your dwelling."

"Though I would by no means deny it," answered Sun Hou (he would not be rude to the stranger, and therefore responded in such a form), "yet I know not how it may be possible, for I have brought with me the key of the house. I pray you, tell me," he continued, "who might this have been?"

"Nay," said Fun, "I know not; I fear I have been impertinent to speak so much."

"No," answered the old man, "I thank you greatly. My ought-to-be-very-much-chastised daughter— But imagine for me who could this person have been?"

"Very reverentially speaking, is there not any whom she loves?"

"And if there should be, how could he get through the key-hole?"

"Had not the door been open in the day?"

"But if he had come in then, where should he have concealed himself?"

"Oh, some will hide themselves in very small corners. I know a youth, a certain Fun, who could hide himself in a good-sized porcelain pot."

"Fun? Fun?— Why that's the very muddy pool of a youth. I had a letter in the morning which informed me so much."

"A letter?—from whom?"—When conversation grows very serious, forms and compliments are a good deal dispensed with, even in China.

" 'Who the black dragon can this be from?' that was the motto. I don't know from whom it came."

"Why that," said Fun, "is the very motto of Fun's own seal. I am well acquainted with

Fun; he and I are inseparable: and from what I know of him, I would wager my brain to a pint of oil, that he brought you the letter himself, and then hid in some corner or jar."

"Oh, it is too true,—it is too true!" cried Sun Hou. "Come with me, Nae-Nae. I will boil my daughter in oil."

"Nay, nay," said Nae-Nae, believing him to be serious,—"Boil only her hands therein."

"Oh, wicked snake of a daughter!" cried Sun Hou, slapping his hands together with great violence. Bang went in the sides of his lantern, and he was fain to put out the light.

"Oh, little wolf of a daughter!" echoed Nae-Nae; and a similar action was attended by a similar result.

Sun Hou and his wife hurried back to their domicile, and Fun, with their daughter, followed. when they reached it they observed that a window was open above; but they saw no person, and no light.

"Alas! alas!" cried the parents, "our wicked daughter has fled. She has gone away with accursed Fun. We shall see her no more."

Sun Hou opened the door, and Nae-Nae entered. Sun Hou had not withdrawn the key, when Fun drew the portal suddenly together and locked it on the outside; in doing so he dexterously contrived to lift up the old gentleman's queue, which was caught in the door as it shut. Sun Hou was fast by his queue. His wife sought in vain for the means of striking a light; the flints and steel were not in their places, and she broke her shins in the search. You may imagine the state of wrath and indignation in which Sun Hou and his wife passed the night.

"Ho," said Fun ere he left the door, "I am the particular friend of Fun,—he begged me to serve him this good turn, and the wine which I drank with him hath made me merry."

"Fun," screamed Sun Hou, "shall be pounded in a mortar for this, and the friend of Fun shall be tied in a sack of snakes."

"Nay," answered Nae-Nae, "they shall laugh the wrong sides of their noses. But, you foolish, old blockhead," said she, " to be duped after this fashion;" and she felt in the dark for Sun Hou's ear, which she twisted severely when she found it.

From the time the young gentleman first accosted the old one, poor Chin Ting, who was in a mortal fright, kept as much out of view as possible. Several times she was on the point of confessing her fault and throwing herself upon the mercy of her father; but she could not gain courage to do so; and when the door was closed, Fun hurried her away as fast as possible. He promised to effect a reconcilation with her parents, if she would become his wife; and having placed her in a sedan, he took her to his house, where many of his friends, whom he had invited to attend his wedding on the propitious evening of the Feast of Lanterns, had been for some time expecting them. At the door they were met by some matrons, his relatives, who assisted Chin Ting out of her sedan, and lifted her over the pan of charcoal placed at the door, agreeably to the marriage custom in the Celestial dominions. They conducted her then to a chamber, and bound up her hair according to the manner in which it is worn by married women; after which she was led by a train of young ladies into the great hall, where she was encouraged to invite the guests to partake of the prepared betel nut. Some other forms were gone through. The most extravagant encomiums were passed upon her beauty: she was compared to the sun, the moon, and stars,—to gold and silver,—to gold and silver fish,—to gold and silver pheasants,—to gems, to flowers, to a dove, to an antelope, to the tea-plant, to the graceful reed, to lanterns and fireworks,—to silkworms,—to rice. The bride-groom, too, was praised as well as congratulated; they made him drink wine; presents were given to both; they wished them honours, long life, and a quiver full of sons. And Chin Ting was the wife of Fun.

The next morning Fun took his beautiful bride to call upon her father. She was disguised as before; and when they reached the house of Sun Hou, Fun at first entered alone, leaving her in her sedan. Fun presented himself with his wonted audacity; but the fury of Sun Hou was so great at seeing, as he supposed, the friend and colleague of Fun,—a person towards whom he had now conceived a greater hatred than even toward Fun himself,—that our hero was almost frightened away, without entering into any explanation. He, however, summoned up forti-tude, and kept bowing and bending with great humility, whilst a storm of abuse was poured up-on him, not from Sun Hou only, but also from his wife Nae-Nae; and when from mere fatigue of these indignant parties, the tempest a little re-laxed, he began in the most conciliatory tones to beg pardon for the unlucky accident of the pre-ceding evening.

"Son of a rotten onion!" cried Sun Hou; "look

at my queue! I could only liberate my head by the loss of my queue. My domestics were obliged to enter my house by placing a ladder to the window."

"Your so-much-dog's-meat of a Fan-Si," responded the youth, "hurried hither this morning, as soon as he remembered his fault, to unlock your majesty's door."

"Wherefore did thy swine-feeding hand turn the key in it last night?" roared Sun Hou.

"Of a truth your scrag-end-of-less-than-nothing was beside himself with wine," humbly ejaculated Fun; "but now, being of clearer sense, the ball of evil which he threw strikes back upon his own nose; and that he may find a salve for the soreness it occasions, he has brought hither a string of pearls, which he solicits your generous condescension to accept."

"Be they real pearls?" said Sun Hou, a little mollified, as he stretched out his hand to receive them.

"Nay, nay," interrupted Nae-Nae, "I fear me they be not real."

"They be real pearls," said Sun Hou. "I forgive you your floutings for this: but how about the loss of my tail?"

"Your most reverence-commanding tail will

grow again," replied Fun; "and meanwhile I have other pearls, of which, with humility, I will entreat your greatly-to-be-knelt for acceptance."

"It is enough," said the old man. "Let this bond of pearls bind us to friendship."

"And may it never be worn out," said Fun.

"Or if it should be," answered Sun Hou, "may it be renewed."

Having so far succeeded, Fun intimated to the old gentleman that he had another favour to request; but begged, before he mentioned it, to be allowed to introduce a lady who was waiting for him below in her sedan, and who he was afraid would feel fatigued. Sun Hou bowed to this with all possible Chinese politeness, and was solicitous to know who the more bright-than-ten thousand-stars lady might be.

"To tell you the truth," answered Fun, "this lady is a bunch of lilies whom I but yesterday took to wife. She is the daughter of a highly respectable old gentleman, for whom I entertain a very cordial esteem."

He conducted the lady into the room. She was still closely veiled. Fourteen minutes elapsed in the usual bows and compliments. Fun then announced the further favour he had to request;—it was a pardon to his friend Fun, and to Fun's wife, Sun Hou's daughter.

"Alas!" cried Sun Hou, "my poor little daughter! I shall never see her more."

"If you will graciously accord pardon to both," said Fun, "I will promise you shall see her this day."

"Wicked Fun," said the father, "shall be strangled, beheaded, poisoned, flayed, and cut in nine million pieces."

"If your worshipful stomach," responded the youth,—the old philosophers held that the stomach is the seat of reason,—"if your worshipful stomach be so ill-minded towards them, I fear you will never find either Fun or your daughter. If you should, Fun, you may be sure, will bribe the mandarins higher for his safety than you will do to get him punished."

"Alas!" exclaimed Sun Hou, "if I may get back my daughter, whom, however, I will well bamboo, I will forgive wicked Fun."

"You must freely pardon your daughter, also, or you will see her no more," responded the youth.

"I will do all things so she shall not be lost to me wholly," said the old man.

"But your virtuous and venerable hand will furnish me with a promise in writing?" asked Fun.

"Anything—anything at all!" replied Sun Hou.

So down they sat and committed the promise to paper. It received the old gentleman's signature. Fun folded it and put it in his vest.

"Most-reverentially-to-be-bowed-before, sir, I am Fun," said Fun.

And Fun bowed lowly and twiddled his queue.

"Most-on-my-knees-to-be-honoured, and more than-my-life-to-be-loved parents, I am Chin Ting," said Chin Ting.

And, bending reverentially, Chin Ting cast back her veil.

The old man raised his staff.—The young man drew out the bond.—The youthful pair fell on their knees, and the aged pair embraced them both.

A CHINESE HERO

One of China's greatest heroes was Han Hsin. He lived in the kingdom of Chin, very many centuries ago. When he was a small boy he showed remarkable wisdom, and, although he was very small of stature, his teachers predicted a great future for him.

One day, when Han was only six years old,

he and another little boy were playing ball, when the ball came down into the deep hole of the mill-stones. They could not get it out at first and the other lad wanted to call for help. Little Han Hsin said, "No, I will think of a plan." Finding a long stick, he began filling the hole with earth. As he poured the earth into the hole, he kept stirring the ball around, thereby keeping it on top of the earth until he could reach it with his hand.

Another time he saw a woman, in rags, jump into a large earthen water-barrel. He was not strong enough to draw her out, and no one was near, so he found a stone and beat with all his strength on the barrel until he made a hole in it near the bottom, and the water running out, the life of the woman was saved. Many such stories, and more wonderful ones, were told of him, and his fame spread all over the kingdom.

In those days every prince had a wise man, or a group of wise men, about him to give him advice regarding the affairs of his kingdom. Han Hsin was presented to his prince by his teachers as worthy of holding such a position, but when the prince and his officers saw how small he was, they laughed and said, "We do not want a child," and would not accept his services.

Han Hsin then went and presented himself at the court of the Prince of Chin Chou. Now, this Prince, Chin Pa, was noted for his strength. It was said of him that, if he tried, he could breathe the roof off the house; also that he could lift himself up by the hair. When he was small he was fed on the milk of the tiger. Thus his strength was not the strength of man.

When Han Hsin was presented to this Prince by his teachers as a wise man and one who could help him make his country strong, he laughed and said, "What can such a boy do? If I hold out my head and tell him to cut it off he has not the strength to do it, even though I stand still and do not resist him. How can there be wisdom in such a small boy? How can such as he help me? He cannot fight for me or wait on me. Take away the child, I do not want him."

The teachers urged the Prince to give the young man a trial and at last he said, "Here is my spear—let him hold it up straight for half a day. If he is strong enough for that, he may find something to do in my service." Alas! Han Hsin could not even for half an hour hold up the great iron spear, and he was driven with laughter and derision from the court.

When the teachers remonstrated with the

Prince he said, "I want no such weaklings in my kingdom."

"But you have made an enemy of him," they urged, and if you do not use him, you should kill him. Although you, our Prince, will not believe us, we know if you let him go he will, in the end, be used by some other kingdom to destroy yours." At this Chin Pa laughed loud and long, but seeing the anxious and serious faces of the teachers he said, "I will take some soldiers and go after him, and if you wish I will kill him."

Now when Han Hsin, in bitterness of heart, was driven from the court he took the road leading to the mountains, and was part way up when, chancing to look back, he saw the mounted band coming. They did not see him, but he knew that they were in search of him. He knew that he could not escape, so he stretched himself out on the side of the hill with his feet toward the top and his head toward the bottom of the hill, and pretended that he was asleep.

When Chin Pa came up and saw him there he smiled to himself and called to his men to remount, and away they went back to the castle, laughing and making merry over the thought that anyone who could sleep in such a position, could rend the kingdom away from their great Prince.

When the teachers heard of the outcome of the pursuit of Han Hsin they were troubled and said, "It is craft and not stupidity—go back again, overtake him and kill him." To please them and for the sport of it, the Prince started out again. By this time Han Hsin had crossed the mountains and was walking on the plains. Again he saw them coming, and looking about he discovered a very ill-smelling hole, and bending over it he exclaimed, as his pursuers came up, "Ah, how sweet, how fragrant!"

This time the Prince declared that Han Hsin was entirely foolish, and he would not kill a fool, for a man who did not know the difference between the sweetly fragrant and the offensive was not one a Prince need fear.

Thus Han Hsin was left to himself, and returned to his own country and village. His own prince, Han Kao Lin, again refused him. At that time this Prince was at war with Chin Pa and was very hard pressed by the latter, and anxious to surround himself with wise men. He could not see, however, how there could be wisdom in such a small man as Han Hsin. But, at last, after much persuasion, he gave a reluctant permission for him to be made leader of the army which was about to set out to attack Chin Pa.

Old pictures show Han Hsin seated on a throne and worshipped by the military men and soldiers under him. They believed that he was to lead them to victory and save their country. It is said that he knew every soldier, and could tell at a glance how many there were in a company passing before him and who were absent from the ranks. He was one of the greatest military leaders, if not the greatest, in Chinese history.

One time, when engaged in war with the Kingdom of Chao, he drove the enemy to the bank of a river, but they got over in their boats and destroyed them on the other side. Feeling secure in the thought that the army of Han Hsin could not cross that night, they made a camp and had a feast. But Han Hsin was not an ordinary man and he commanded every man to get a board of some kind and in the darkness to swim across quietly. This they did, and fell upon the merry camp and won a great victory.

Another time Han Hsin insisted on camping on the shore of the great river. His officers and men protested, and said that he was not leaving any path for retreat in case of defeat, as they had no ships or bridges and few could swim so far. All the comfort they could get was his reply, "When defeat comes we will discuss the question." The enemy were seen coming upon them from the front, and then Han Hsin called to his men to fight for their lives, for death was certainly behind them in the river, but, if they fought bravely, they could defeat the enemy in front. This they did with great slaughter.

At another time, when fighting with the great Chin Pa, of the Kingdom of Chin, the latter shut up all but one of the roads over the mountains and awaited Han Hsin in ambuscade in a very narrow place, the only one where it seemed possible for him to get over the mountains. He did not even then know the military master he had to deal with in Han Hsin, as it was still early in the war. Han Hsin sent out his spies, disguised as countrymen, and learned the condition of things. So, calling upon his men to make a lot of bags, even turning their clothes into bags, his army set out.

On reaching the steepest place in ascending the mountains, he commanded the army to halt and fill the bags with earth. This place was not guarded, as it was supposed to be impossible of ascent. During the night, however, Han Hsin ordered an advance, and, using the bags to make a series of steps, his army went quickly up and over to the other side, to the rear of Chin Pa's army. Here Han Hsin attacked the enemy in force and easily put them to flight. Later they recovered themselves and in many battles afterward between these two great generals neither could obtain any great advantage.

Now Han Hsin had a friend and helper in Chang Lang, a literary man who was wise and safe to trust, and who often helped him in his plans. They talked over the situation, and Chang Lang said that the strength of Chin Pa was in a company of three thousand soldiers who were all related to each other, and whose officers were also of the same clan. In some way that company must be disbanded or Han Hsin never would win the final victory. Many plans were formed, but the soldiers of the clan seemed to possess charmed lives.

At last Chang Lang came one night to the tent of Han Hsin and said, "I have found a way, and, as there is a fine wind and it is on the eve of battle, I will try my new scheme." He then produced a large kite, the first ever made, and disclosed his plan. All these years Han Hsin had remembered how Chin Pa had laughed at his small stature, but he was that night to show him that though small, he was formidable as an enemy.

Some of his officers were called in and fastened him by ropes to the kite and then let go. Gradually the kite ascended, and, in the twilight, appeared high over the camp of the three thousand soldiers. They were filled with terror, for never before had such a thing been seen or heard of. It was dark enough to prevent them from seeing Han Hsin at the height and distance he was from them. The kite came to rest for a few moments, and they heard a voice say, "You all have old and young in your homes. Why do you not go home to them? If you stay on, you will some day all be killed; then who will worship at the grave of your fathers and hand down the name?"

The men said, "It is a voice of a god, a warning, let us depart at once," and that night they left the camp.

The battle next day was terrific, but in the end Han Hsin won a great victory. When urged to kill his old enemy he said, "No, let him go, for he will kill himself, and that will be better." So, Chin Pa was set at liberty and started with his army to return south. The battle had been near a river and Han Hsin knew that Chin Pa must cross it on his retreat. So, before the battle was fought, Han Hsin had written, in honey, on a big stone slab near the ford, these four words. "Heaven Destroy Hsiang Yi." The last two words were Chin Pa's name. A swarm of ants scenting the honey crawled up to eat it, and thus outlined the characters very distinctly.

When Chin Pa came over the river and saw the stone with the four large characters he said, "Woe is me, even the worms and ants know that Heaven has deserted me. I will kill myself." And then and there, almost in sight of his adversary, the man he had regarded with contempt, he killed himself.

Thus ended a strife of nearly twenty years between two kingdoms, and Han Hsin came to be the Prince of his kingdom. Often during the time of kite-flying in China, away in the heavens one sees a kite in the shape of an old-time warrior, and few of the many beautiful and fancy kites to be seen have such an interesting story. The kite has come to be, in Western lands, merely an amusement, but in China, where it was probably invented, it ever carries with the message, "Strength of mind is greater than strength of body."

THE WILD GOOSE AND THE SPARROW

The great Chinese sage, Confucius, had a son-in-law, Kung Yeh Chang, who understood better than any one before or since his day the habit of birds. So much time and study did he give to them that tradition says he understood all bird language and many stories are told of him in this connection. He built a beautiful pavilion in his garden, which was rich in flowers, trees, shrubs, and ponds, so that the birds loved to gather there; thus he was able to spend many delightful hours in their company listening to their wise and unwise talk.

Many of these conversations have been handed down the past two thousand years in the wonderful folklore of China, and from these one can see the influence they have had on the customs and traditions of the people.

Among the Chinese the wild goose has the reputation for having more virtues and wisdom than any other bird. This is brought out in the following story. One day, while Kung Yeh

Chang was resting in his pavilion, a small house-sparrow lit in a tree near-by and commenced singing and chattering. A little later a wild goose dropped down by the pond for a drink. Hardly had he taken a sip when the little sparrow called out, "Who are you? Where are you going?" To this the goose did not reply and the sparrow became angry and asked again, "Who are you, that you should be so proud and lofty you cannot pay attention to my questions? Why do you consider me beneath your notice?" and still the goose did not answer. Then, indeed, was the little sparrow furious. In a loud, shrill voice, he said, "Every one listens to me! Again I ask, who are you with your lofty airs? Tell me or I will fly at you," and he put his head up, and spread his wings, and tried to look very large and fierce.

By this time the goose had finished drinking, and looking up he said, "Don't you know that in a big tree with many branches and large leaves the cicadas love to gather and make a noise? I could not hear you distinctly. You also know the saying of the Ancients, 'If you stand on a mountain and talk to the people in the valley they cannot hear you,' " and the wild goose took another drink.

How the little sparrow chattered and sputtered, shook his wings, and at last said, "In what way are you, with your long neck and short tail, better than I? In what is your value greater? Tell me, and if you can prove it you shall be my teacher. What, for instance, do you know of the great world? Now I can go into people's houses, hide in the rafters under their windows, see their books and pictures, what they have to eat and what they do. I can hear all the family secrets, know all that goes on in the family and state. I know who are happy and who are sad. I know all the quarrels and all the gossip. All the other birds are glad to see me because I can tell them the latest news, and I know just how to tell it to produce the best effect. So you see that I know much that you, with your great stupid body, can never hope to know."

"We consider," said the wild goose, "that the highest law of virtue and good is to give others an equal chance with ourselves, or even to give them the first choice. Because of this we always fly either in the shape of the character 'Man,' or the figure one. No one takes advantage of the other. We believe in the 'Three Bonds,' i. e., Prince and Minister, Husband and Wife,

Father and Son. Also in the five virtues,—
Benevolence, Righteousness, Propriety, Knowledge, and Truth. With us, if the male bird dies,
the female flies alone; if the female dies the male
flies alone; if both parents die their young fly
alone for three years. We have our unchanging
customs of going north in the spring and south
in the winter. People come to depend on us,
and make ready for either their spring work or
the cold of winter. Thus, while we have not
known the family or state skeletons and the
gossip of the women and servants, we are a help
to man.

"Now, you have no laws binding you. As a
family, you sparrows are selfish; you gossip,
chatter, steal, and drive away every one else,
only thinking of your own good. Even among
yourselves you quarrel. Because of these things
you are treated with contempt and looked lightly
upon by all. Indeed, so much so that you are a
by-word. Now, we are respected and held up
as models. Do you not hear parents and
teachers tell their children and scholars to come
and go quietly by themselves to and from school;
to go straight ahead without looking to the right
or left; not to gather in groups and chatter like
house-sparrows? Do not the respectable people

do the same on the street and in the house? Is there not a proverb that 'There are many people without the wisdom and virtues of the wild goose'? You do, indeed, chatter about small affairs like foolish women and girls and thus are beneath my notice and I bid you good-day."

All this time the poor little sparrow was trembling with rage, and so great was it that she could not fly away nor keep her hold on the branch of the tree, and so she fell to the ground, and thus she died.

Kung Yeh Chang exclaimed as he looked at her and then at the goose away in the distance, "Ai ya (sad, sad), most of mankind are like the sparrow, but the truly superior man will be like the wild goose and follow the rules of the Three Bonds and Five Virtues."

THE COUNTRY OF GENTLEMEN

More than a thousand years ago there lived an Empress of China, who was a very bold and obstinate woman. She thought she was powerful enough to do anything. One day, she even gave orders, that every kind of flower throughout the country was to be out in full bloom on a certain day. Being a woman herself, she thought that women would govern the empire much better than men; so she actually had examinations for women and gave them all the important posts. This made a great many men extremely angry; especially a young man named Tang, who was very clever and had taken many prizes. He said he couldn't live in such a country any more; and sailed away with an uncle of his and another friend on a long voyage to distant parts of the world. They visited many extraordinary nations; in one of which, the people all had heads of dogs; in another, they flew about like birds; in another, they had enormously long arms with which they reached down into the water to catch fish. Then there was the country of tall men, where everybody was about twenty feet in height; the country of dwarfs where the people were only one foot in height, and their funny little children were not more than four inches. In another place, the people all had large holes in the middle of their bodies; and rich persons were carried about by servants who pushed long sticks through the holes. After a time, they came to a land which they were told was the Country of Gentlemen. They went ashore, and walked out to the capital. There they found the people buying and selling, and strange to say they were all talking the Chinese language. They also noticed that everybody was very polite, and the foot-passengers in the streets were very careful to step aside and make room for one another. In the market-place they saw a man who was buying things at a shop. Holding the things in his hand, the man was saying to the shopkeeper, "My dear sir, I really cannot take these excellent goods at the absurdly low price you are asking. If you will oblige me by doubling the amount, I shall do myself the honour of buying them; otherwise I shall know for certain that you do not wish to do business with me today." The shopkeeper replied, "Excuse me, sir, I am already very much ashamed at having asked you so much for these goods; they really are not worth more than half. If you insist upon paying such a high price, I must really beg you, with all possible respect, to go and buy in some other shop." At this, the man who wanted to buy got rather angry, and said that trade could not be carried on at all if all the profit was on one side and all the loss on the other, adding that the shopkeeper was not going to catch him in a trap like that. After a lot more talk, he put down the full price on the counter, but only took half the things. Of course the shopkeeper would not agree to this, and they would have gone on arguing forever had not two old gentlemen who happened to be passing stepped aside and arranged the matter for them by deciding that the purchaser was to pay the full price but only to receive three-quarters of the goods. Tong heard this sort of thing going on at every shop he passed. It was always the buyer who wanted to give as much as possible, and the seller to take as little. In one case the shopkeeper called after a customer who was hurrying away with the goods he had bought and said, "Sir, sir, you have paid me too much, you have paid me too much." "Pray don't mention it," replied the customer, "but oblige me by keeping the money for another day when I come again to buy some more of your excellent goods." "No, no," answered the shopkeeper, "you don't catch old birds with chaff; that trick was played upon me last year by a gentleman who left some money with me, and to this day I have never set eyes upon him again though I have tried all I can to find out where he lives." But soon they had to say good-bye to this wonderful country and started once more upon their voyage. They next came to a very strange land where the people did not walk but moved about upon small clouds of different colours, about half a foot from the ground. Meeting with an old priest, who seemed rather a queer man, Tang asked him to be kind enough to explain the meaning of the little clouds upon which the people rode. "Ah sir," said the priest, "these clouds show what sort of a heart is inside the persons who are riding on them. People can't choose their own colours; clouds striped like a rainbow are the best; yellow are the second best, and black are the worst of all." Thanking the old man, they passed on and among those who were riding on clouds of green, red, blue and other colours, they saw a dirty beggar riding on a striped cloud. They were much astonished at this because the old priest had told them that the striped cloud was the best. "I see why that was," said Tang, "the old rascal had a striped cloud himself." Just then the people in the street began to fall back, leaving a passage in the middle; and by and by they saw a very grand officer pass along in great state with a long procession of servants carrying red umbrellas, gongs, and other things. They tried to see what colour his cloud was, but to their disappointment it was covered up with a curtain of red silk. "Oho!" said Tang, "this gentleman has evidently got such a bad colour for his cloud that he is ashamed to let it be seen. I wish we had clouds like these in our country so that we could tell good people from bad by just looking at them. I don't think there would be so many wicked men about then." Soon after this, news reached them that the Empress who had been so troublesome in their own country had been obliged to give up the throne. So they went no further on their travels but turned their ship round towards home, where their families were very glad to see them again.

CONTENTMENT IN HUMBLENESS

One day, an old priest stopped at a wayside inn to rest, spread out his mat, and sat down his bag. Soon afterwards, a young fellow of the neighbourhood also arrived at the inn; he was a farm-labourer and wore short clothes, not a long robe like the priest and men who read books. He took a seat near to the priest and the two were soon laughing and talking together. By and by, the young man cast a glance at his own rough dress and said with a sigh, "See, what a miserable wretch I am." "You seem to be well fed and healthy enough," replied the priest; "why in the middle of our pleasant chat do you suddenly complain of being a miserable wretch?" "What pleasure can I find," retorted the young man, "in this life of mine, working every day as I do from early morn to late at night? I should like to be a great general and win battles, or to be a rich man and have fine food and wine, and listen to good music, or to be a great man at court and help our Emperor and bring prosperity to my family;—that is what I call pleasure. I want to rise in the world, but here I am a poor farm-labourer; if you don't call that miserable wretch-edness, what is it?" He then began to get sleepy, and while the landlord was cooking a dish of millet-porridge, the priest took a pillow out of his bag and said to the young man, "Lay your head on this and all your wishes will be granted." The pillow was made of porcelain; it was round like a tube, and open at each end. When the young man put his head down towards the pillow, one of the openings seemed so large and bright inside that he got in, and soon found himself at his own home. Shortly afterwards he married a beautiful girl, and began to make money. He now wore fine clothes and spent his time in study. In the following year he passed his examination and was made a magistrate; and in two or three years he had risen to be Prime Minister. For a long time the Emperor trusted him in everything, but the day came when he got into trouble; he was accused of treason and sentenced to death. He was taken with several other criminals to the place of execution; he was made to kneel on both knees, and the executioner approached with his sword. Too terrified to feel the blow, he opened his eyes, to find himself in the inn. There was the priest with his head on his bag; and there was the landlord still stirring the porridge, which was not quite ready. After eating his meal in silence, he got up and bowing to the priest, said, "I thank you, sir, for the lesson you have taught me; I know now what it means to be a great man!" With that, he took his leave and went back to his work.

MONKEY THAT BECAME KING

Long, long ago, on the top of a mountain called the Flower-and-Fruit Mountain, there lay all by itself a square-shaped stone egg. No one knew what bird had laid it, or how it had got there; no one ever saw it, for there was nobody there to see. The egg lay all by itself on some green grass, until one day it split with a crack, and out came a stone monkey, a monkey whose body was of shining polished stone. Before long, this wonderful stone monkey was surrounded by a crowd of monkeys and other animals, chattering to one another as hard as they could. By and by they seemed to have settled something in their minds, and one of them came forward and asked the stone monkey to be their king. This post he accepted at once, having indeed already thrown out hints that he thought himself quite fit to rule over them.

Soon after this, he determined to travel in search of wisdom, and to see the world. He went down the mountain, until he came to the sea-shore, where he made himself a raft, and sailed away. Reaching the other side of the grate ocean, he found his way to the abode of a famous magician, and persuaded the magician to teach him all kinds of magical tricks. He learned to make himself invisible, to fly up into the sky, and to jump many miles at a single jump. At last he began to think himself better and stronger than anybody else, and determined to make himself Lord of the Sky.

. . . .

"Have you heard of the new "Monkey King?" said the Dragon prince to the Lord Buddha one day, as they were sitting together in the palace of the sky. "No," answered the Lord Buddha. "What is there to hear about him?" "He has been doing a lot of mischief," replied the Dragon prince. He has learnt all kinds of magical tricks, and knows more than anybody else in the whole world. He now means to turn the Lord of the Sky out of his place, and be Lord of the Sky himself. I promised I would ask you to help us against this impudent stone monkey. If you will be good enough to do so, I feel sure we should conquer him." The Lord Buddha promised to do his best, and the two went together to the cloud palace of the Lord of the Sky, where they found the stone monkey misbehaving himself, and insulting everybody who dared to interfere with him. The Lord Buddha stepped forward, and in a quiet voice said to him, "What do you want?" "I want," answered the stone monkey, "to be Lord of the Sky. I could manage things much better than they are managed now. See how I can jump." Then the stone monkey jumped a big jump. In a moment he was out of sight, and in another moment he was back again. "Can you do that?" he asked the Lord Buddha; at which the Lord Buddha only smiled and said, "I will make a bargain with you. You shall come outside the palace with me and stand upon my hand. Then, if you can jump out of my hand, you shall be Lord of the Sky, as you wish to be; but if you cannot jump out of my hand, you shall be sent down to earth, and never be allowed to come up to the sky any more." The stone monkey laughed loudly when he heard this, and said, "Jump out of your hand, Lord Buddha! Why of course I can easily do that." So they went outside the palace, and the Lord Buddha put down his hand, and the stone monkey stepped on to it. He then gave one great jump, and again he was away far out of sight. On and on he went in his jump, until he came to the end of the earth. There he stopped; and while he was chuckling to himself that he would soon be Lord of the Sky, he caught sight of five great red pillars standing on the very edge with nothing but empty space beyond; and now he thought he would leave a mark to show how far he had really jumped. So he scratched a mark on one of the pillars, meaning to bring the Lord Buddha there to see it for himself. When he had done this, he took another big jump, and in the twinkling of an eye he was back again in the Lord Buddha's hand. "When are you going to begin to jump?" the Lord Buddha asked, as the monkey stepped down on to the ground. "When!" cried the monkey sarcastically. "Why, I have jumped, —jumped to the very end of the earth. If you want to know how far I have been, you have only to get on my back, and I'll take you there to see. There are five red pillars there, and I've left a mark on one of them." "Look here, monkey," the Lord Buddha said, holding out his hand. "Look at this." The stone monkey looked. On one of the fingers of the Lord Buddha's hand there was the very mark which he himself had made on the red pillar. "You see," said the Lord Buddha; "the whole world lies in my hand. You could never have jumped out of it. When you jumped, and thought you were out of sight, my hand was under you all the time. No one, not even a stone monkey, can ever get beyond my reach. Now go down to earth, and learn to keep your proper place."

THE TAOIST'S GARDEN.

In ancient times there lived a retired Taoist scholar whose name was Hsuan-wei. He never married, but dwelt alone, yet his companions were books, and flowers his little friends. If he had any enemies, they were frost and wind and blight and mildew. Three seasons brought him joy and one sorrow. Love to him meant the gentle opening of rose-petals, and death their fall. The neighbours never troubled about him, for how could there be scandal between a man and flowers? No woman ever plundered his garden and desecrated his Temple of Abiding Peace. In fine, he was the happiest man that ever lived.

Then something came to pass. It was "blue night," and the garden never looked whiter underneath the moon. And every tree melted the spirit of a tree peering between its luminous leaves. The Wu t'ung whispered to the maple, and the maple passed the story round to the mountain pine of the phoenix that augustly condescended to rest in its branches—some long-forgotten spring. Only the old willow stood apart and said nothing, for the willow is a wizard, and the older he gets the more crabbed and silent he becomes.

The owner of the garden stood spell-bound in the moonlight. Suddenly a blue shadow flitted shyly from among the flowers and a lady in a long robe of palest blue came towards him and bowed. "I live not far from here," said she, "and in passing to visit my August Aunt I felt a longing to rest in your beautiful garden."

The wondering philospher stammered his consent, and instantly a band of pretty girls appeared, some carrying flowers and some willow boughs. According to etiquette an introduction became necessary.

Then a girl in green announced herself: "I am called Aspen," and, pointing to a girl in white, "her name is Plum," to one in purple, "she is called Peach," and so she went on till the last, a little maid in crimson, who was called Pomegranate. The Lady Wind, who, she explained, was their maternal Aunt eighteen times removed, had promised them a visit which for some reason she had delayed. As tonight's moon was unusually bright, they had decided to visit her instead. Just at that instant the Lady Wind was announced, and, with a great fluttering of many-coloured silks, the girls trooped out to greet her and one and all implored her to stay with them in the garden. Meanwhile, Mr. Hsuan-wei had discreetly retired into the shadow. But when the August Aunt asked who the owner was he stepped boldly into the moonlight and saw a lady of surpassing grace with a certain gauzy floating appearance like gossamer. But her words chilled him, for they were like

the cold breath stirring the leaves of a black forest, and so he shivered. However, with the true
politeness of a Chinese host, he invited her into
his contemptible Pavilion of Abiding Peace,
where he was astonished to find a magnificent
banquet already prepared.

So they feasted and sang, and I am sorry to
say that many cups went round, and the Lady
Wind became both critical and extravagant.
She condemned two unfortunate singers to pay
forfeit by drinking a full goblet apiece, but her
hands shook so as she held the goblets out that
they slipped from her grasp and fell with a crash
to the floor. And much wine was spilled over
poor little Pomegranate, who had appeared for
the first time in her new embroidered crimson
robe. Pomegranate, being a girl of spirit, was
naturally annoyed, and, telling her sisters they
could court their Aunt themselves, she blushed
herself off.

The Lady Wind, in a great rage, cried out
that she had been insulted, and, though they all
tried to calm her, she gathered her robe
about her and out of the door she flew off hiss-
ing to the east. Then all the girls came before
their flower philosopher and bowed and swayed
sorrowfully and said farewell, and, floating

through the portals, vanished into the white parterres around; and when Mr. Hsuan-wei looked, lo, the Temple of Abiding Peace was empty as all temples of its kind should be. And he sat down to wonder if it was a dream. For every trace of the feast was gone and yet a faint subtle fragrance lingered as though some gracious and flowerlike presence had once been a guest.

Next night, when strolling in his garden, he was suddenly surrounded by his little friends. They were all busy discussing the conduct of Pomegranate and urging her to apologise to the August Aunt eighteen times removed. It was evident that they went in fear of her since last night's unfortunate revel. But little red Pomegranate would have no truck with Aunt Wind, who had spoilt her nice new robe. "Here is one who will protect us from any harm," she cried, pointing to the surrounded form of Mr. Hsuan-wei. So they told him how each year they were injured by spiteful gales and how Aunt Wind had to some extent protected them.

Mr. Hsuan-wei was sorely puzzled: "How can this contemptible one afford protection?" he asked. Pomegranate explained. It was such a very little thing required of him—just to prepare a crimson flag embroidered with sun, moon, and stars in gold and hoist it east of the garden at dawn on the first morning of each new year, then all hurricanes would pass them by. Accordingly, he promised, and the next day saw him stitching golden stars on a crimson background. And he rose early, an hour before the dawn, upon the appointed day and set his flag duly towards the east in the breath of a light east wind. Suddenly a great storm gathered and broke. The world rocked. The air was dark with flying stones and whirling dust. The giants of the forest cracked, others were overwhelmed. But in Mr. Hsuan-wei's garden there was a deep calm. Not a flower stirred. Then in a flash he understood. His little friends whom he had saved from destruction were the souls of his little flowers. That night, when the moon was midway, they came to him with garlands of peach and plum blossom whose taste conferred the beauty of everlasting youth. Mr. Hsuan-wei partook of the petals and straightway the lingering drift of old sorrows from the days of his ignorance melted like snow from his heart. And with it went all the pathetic rubbish that even a flower philospher allows to accumulate. He became young and divinely empty, yet in his soul pulsed new life. "Soon afterwards," says the ancient chronicle, "he attained to a knowledge of the True Way, and shared the immortality of the Genii."

THE FLOWER NYMPHS
Told by
CHIN YUN

At the lower temple on Mount Lao the camellias are twenty feet in height, and many spans in circumference. The peonies are more than ten feet high; and when the flowers are in bloom the effect is that of gorgeous tapestry.

There was a Mr. Huang, of Chiao-chow, who built himself a house at that spot, for the purposes of study; and one day he saw from his window a young lady dressed in white wandering about amongst the flowers. Reflecting that she could not possibly belong to the monastery, he went out to meet her, but she had already disappeared. After this he freuquently observed her, and once hid himself in a thick-foliaged bush, waiting for her to come. By-and-by she appeared, bringing with her another young lady dressed in red, who, as he noticed from his distant, point of observation, was an exceedingly good-looking girl. When they approached nearer, the young lady in the red dress ran back, saying "There is a man here!" whereupon Mr. Huan jumped out upon them, and away they went in a scare, with their skirts and long sleeves fluttering in the breeze, and perfuming the air around. Huang pursued them as far as a low wall, where they suddenly vanished from his gaze. In great distress at thus losing the fair creatures, he took a pencil and wrote upon a tree the following lines:—

> The pangs of love my heart enthrall
>   As I stand opposite this wall.
> I dread some hateful tyrant's power,
>   With none to save you in that hour.

Returning home he was absorbed in his own thoughts, when all at once the young lady walked in, and he rose up joyfully to meet her. "I thought you were a brigand," said his visitor, smiling; "you nearly frightened me to death. I did not know you were a great scholar whose acquaintance I now hope to have the honour of making." Mr. Huang asked the young lady her name, etc., to which she replied, "My name is Hsiang-yu, and I belong to P'ingk'ang-hsiang; but a magician has condemned me to remain on this hill much against my own inclination." "Tell me his name," cried Huang, "and

I'll soon set you free." "There is no need for that," answered the young lady; "I suffer no injury from him, and the place is not an inconvenient one for making the acquaintance of such worthy gentlemen as yourself." Huang then inquired who was the young lady in red, and she told him that her name was Chiang-hsueh, and that they were half-sisters; "and now," added she, "I will sing you a song; but please don't laugh at me." She then began as follows:—

> In pleasant company the hours fly fast,
>   And through the window daybreak peeps at last.
> Ah, would that, like the swallow and his mate,
>   To live together were our happy fate.

Huang here grasped her hand and said, "Beauty without and intellect within—enough to make a man love you and forget all about death, only one day's absence being like the separation of a thousand miles. I pray you come again whenever an opportunity may present itself." From this time the young lady would frequently walk in to have a chat, but would never bring her sister with her in spite of all Mr. Huang's entreaties. Huang thought they weren't friends, but Hsiang said her sister did not care for society in the same way that she herself did, promising at the same time to try and persuade her to come at some future day. On the evening of the Feast of Lanterns, Hsiang-yu arrived in a melancholy frame of mind, and told Huang that he was wanting more when he couldn't even keep what he had got; "for to-morrow," said she, "we part." Huang asked what she meant; and then, wiping away her tears with her sleeve, Hsiang-yu declared it was destiny, and that she couldn't well tell him. "Your former prophecy," continued she, "has come too true; and now it may well be said of me——

> Fallen into the tyrant's power,
>   With none to save me in that hour."

Huang again tried to question her, but she would tell him nothing; and by-and-by she rose and took her leave. This seemed very strange; however, next day a visitor came, who, after wandering round the garden, was much taken with a white peony, which he dug up and carried away with him. Huang now awaked to the fact that Hsiang-yu was a flower nymph, and became very disconsolate in consequence of what had happened; but when he subsequently heard that the peony only lived a few days after being taken away, he wept bitterly, and composed an elegy in fifty stanzas, besides going daily to the hole from which it had been taken, and watering the ground with his tears. One day, as he was returning thence, he espied the young lady of the red clothes also wiping away her tears alongside the hole and immediately walked back gently toward her. She did not run away, and Huang grasping her sleeve, joined with her in her lamentations. When these were concluded he invited her to his house, and then she burst out with a sigh, saying, "Alas! that the sister of my early years should be thus suddenly taken from me. Hearing you, Sir, mourn as you did, I have also been moved to tears. Those you shed have sunk down deep to the realms below, and may perhaps succeed in restoring her to us; but the sympathies of the dead are destroyed for ever, and how then can she laugh and talk with us again?" "My luck is bad," said Huang, "that I should injure those I love, neither can I have the good fortune to draw towards me another such a beauty. But tell me, when I often sent messages by Hsiang-yu to you, why did you not come?" "I knew, replied she, "what nine young fellows out of ten are; but I did not know what you were." She then took leave, Husang telling her how dull he felt without Hsiang-yu, and begging her to come again. For some days she did not appear; and Huang remained in a state of great melancholy, tossing and turning on his bed and wetting the pillow with his tears, until one night he got up, put on his clothes, and trimmed the lamp; and having called for pen and ink, he composed the following lines:—

On my cottage roof the evening rain-drops beat;
I draw the blind and near the window take my seat.
To my longing gaze no loved one appears;
Drip, drip, drip, drip: fast flow my tears.

This he read aloud; and when he had finished, a voice outside said, "You want some one to cap your verses there!" Listening attentively, he knew it was Chiang-hsueh and opening the door he let her in. She looked at his stanza and added impromptu——

She is no longer in the room;
A single lamp relieves the gloom;
One solitary man is there;
He and his shadow make a pair.

As Huang read these words his tears fell fast; and then, turning to Chiang-hsueh, he upbraided her for not having been to see him. "I can't come so often as Hsiang-yu did," replied she, "but only now and then when you are very

dull." After this she used to drop in occasionally and Huang said Hsiang-yu was his beloved
wife, and she his dear friend, always trying to
find out every time she came which flower in the
garden she was, that he might bring her home
with him, and save her from the fate of Hsiang-
yu. "The old earth should not be disturbed,"
said she, "and it would not do any good to tell
you. If you couldn't keep your wife always
with you, how will you be sure of keeping a
friend?" Huang, however, paid no heed to
this, and seizing her arm, led her out into the garden, where he stopped at every peony and asked
if this was the one; to which Chiang-hsueh made
no reply, but only put her hand to her mouth
and laughed.

At New Year's, during the Feast of Lanterns Huang went home, and a couple of months
afterwards he dreamt that Chiang-hsueh came
to tell him she was in great trouble, begging him
to hurry off as soon as possible to her rescue.
When he woke up, he thought his dream a very
strange one; and ordering his servant and horses
to be ready, started at once for the hills. There
he found that the priests were about to build a
new room; and finding a camellia in the way,
the contractor had given orders that it should be

cut down. Huang now understood his dream, and immediately took steps to prevent the destruction of the flower. That night Chiang-hsueh came to thank him, and Huang laughed and said, "It serves you right for not telling me which you were. Now I know you, and if you don't come and see me, I'll get a firebrand and make it hot for you." "That's just why I didn't tell you before," replied she. "The presence of my dear friend," said Huang, after a pause, "makes me think more of my lost wife. It is long since I have mourned for her. Shall we go and bemoan her loss together?" So they went off and shed many a tear on the spot where formerly Hsiang-yu had stood, until at last Chiang-hsueh wiped her eyes and said it was time to go. A few evenings later Huang was sitting alone, when suddenly Chiang-hsueh entered, her face radiant with smiles. "Good news!" cried she; "the Flower-God, moved by your tears, has granted Hsiang-yu a return to life. Huang was overjoyed, and asked when she would come; to which Chiang-hsueh replied, that she could not say for certain, but that it would not be long. "I came here on your account," said Huang; "don't let me be duller than you can help." "All right," answered she, and then went away, not returning for the next two evenings. Huang then went into the garden and threw his arms around her plant, entreating her to come and see him, though without eliciting any response. He accordingly went back, and began twisting up a torch, when all at once in she came, and snatching the torch out of his hand, threw it away, saying, "You're a bad fellow, and I don't like you, and I sha'n't have any more to do with you." However, Huang soon succeeded in pacifying her, and by-and-by in walked Hsiang-yu herself. Huang now wept tears of joy as he seized her hand, and drawing Chiang-hsueh towards them, the three friends mingled their tears together. They then sat down and talked over the miseries of separation, Huang meanwhile noticing that Hsiang-yu seemed to be unsubstantial, and that when he grasped her hand his fingers seemed to close only on themselves, and not as in the days gone by. This Hsiang-yu explained, saying, "When I was a flower-nymph I had a body; but now I am only the disembodied spirit of that flower. Do not regard me as a reality, but rather as an apparition seen in a dream." "You have come at the nick of time," cried Chiang-hsueh; "your husband there was getting troublesome." Hsiang-yu now instructed Hsuang to take a little powdered white-berry and mixing it with some sulphur to pour out a libation to her, adding, "This day next year I will return your kindness." The young ladies then went away, and next day Huang observed the shoots of a young peony growing where Hsiang-yu had once stood. So he made the libation as she told him, and had the plant very carefully tended, even building a fence all round to protect it. Hsiang-yu came to thank him for this, and he proposed that the plant should be removed to his own home; but to this she would not agree, "for," said she, "I am not very strong, and could not stand being transplanted. Besides, all things have their appointed place; and as I was not originally intended for your home, it might shorten my life to be sent there. We can love each other very well here." Huang then asked why Chiang-hsueh did not come; to which Hsiang-yu replied that they must make her, and proceeded with him into the garden, where, after picking a blade of grass, she measured upwards from the roots of Chiang-hsueh's plant to a distance of four feet six inches, at which point she stopped and Huang began to scratch a mark on the place with his nails. At that moment Chiang-hsueh came from behind the plant, and in mock anger cried out, "You hussy you! what do you aid that wretch for?" "Don't be angry, my dear," said Hsiang-yu; "help me to amuse him for a year only, and then you sha'n't be bothered any more." So they went on, Huang watching the plant thrive, and by the time the Feast of Lanterns came it was over two feet in height. He then went home, giving the priests a handsome present, and bidding them take great care of it. Next year, in the fourth moon, he returned and found upon the plant a bud just ready to break; and as he was walking round, the stem shook violently as if it would snap, and suddenly the bud opened into a flower as large as a plate, disclosing a beautiful maiden within, sitting upon one of the pistils, and only a few inches in height. In the twinkling of an eye she had jumped out, and lo! it was Hsiang-yu. "Through the wind and the rain I have waited for you," cried she; "why have you come so late?" They then went into the house, where they found Chiang-hsueh already arrived, and sat down to enjoy themselves as they had done in former times. Shortly afterwards Huang's wife died, and he took up his abode at Mount Lao for good and all. The peonies were at that time as large round as one's arm; and whenever Huang went to look at them he always said, "Some day my spirit will be there by your sides"; to which the two girls used to reply with a laugh, and say, "Mind you don't forget." Ten years after these events, Huang became dangerously ill, and his son, who had come to see him, was very much distressed about him. "I am about to be born," cried his father; "I am not going to die. Why do you weep?" He also told the priests that if later on they should see a red shoot, with five leaves, thrusting itself forth alongside of the peony, that would be himself. This was all he said, and his son proceeded to convey him home, where he died immediately on arrival. Next year a shoot did come up exactly as he had mentioned; and the priests, struck by the coincidence, watered it and supplied it with earth. In three years it was a tall plant, and a good span in circumference, but without flowers. When the old priest died, the others took no care of it; and as it did not flower they cut it down. The white peony then faded and died; and before the next Feast of Lanterns the camellia was dead too.

THE END